THE CORPS OF THE BARE-BONED PLANE

The
CORPS
of the
BARE-BONED
PLANE

POLLY HORVATH

FARRAR STRAUS GIROUX / NEW YORK

www.fsgkidsbooks.com

Library of Congress Cataloging-in-Publication Data
Horvath, Polly.
    The Corps of the Bare-Boned Plane / Polly Horvath.— 1st ed.
        p.   cm.
    Summary: When their parents are killed in a train accident, cousins
Meline and Jocelyn, who have little in common, are sent to live with their
wealthy, eccentric, and isolated Uncle Marten on his island off the coast of
British Columbia, where they are soon joined by other oddly disconnected
and troubled people.
    ISBN-13: 978-0-374-31553-5
    ISBN-10: 0-374-31553-1
    [1. Death—Fiction.   2. Grief—Fiction.   3. Uncles—Fiction.
4. Cousins—Fiction.   5. Airplanes—Fiction.   6. Islands—Fiction.
7. British Columbia—Fiction.]   I. Title.

PZ7.H79224 Co 2007
[Fic]—dc22
                                                        2006041281

To Claudia Logan, my best friend

THE CORPS OF THE BARE-BONED PLANE

MELINE

IT WAS A DARK NIGHT when I left my home in Hyannis Port. A social worker came to the door for me. My twenty-four-year-old babysitter, Tiffany, blond, recently dropped out of college and at loose ends, not terribly bright, but well heeled like most of the girls in this town, was too excited by it all to leave. She stood behind me while the social worker told me that my parents had been killed in a train wreck in Zimbabwe along with my aunt and uncle. That Jocelyn, my cousin, had survived and was on her way to my Uncle Marten's house in British Columbia. That he had been named legal guardian for both of us. Jocelyn was sixteen and I was fifteen, and he would take us in until we were old enough to go to college.

"Or whatever," said Tiffany, who had decided to join in at this point, shrugging. Up until that moment she had been breathing on my neck adenoidally with her mouth open. Her breath felt as if it had condensed there, and when I put my hand up unconsciously to wipe off my neck I accidentally hit her in the mouth. She didn't yelp with pain or take a step back but continued breathing loudly as if in a trance, completely mesmerized by the recent developments and my sudden misfortune. I had a feeling that when she got home she would phone all her friends and say, "It was so cool, her parents were, like, wiped out, and this woman came and, like, totally took her away. And like, I get paid now from the estate. Isn't that totally weird?"

You would think that when you have just found out your parents have been killed, you wouldn't be thinking things like this, catty thoughts about your babysitter, that you would be beyond noticing, but although it's as if some part of you is suddenly unplugged, all your old responses stand you in good stead. You continue to be yourself, to think the sorts of thoughts you have always thought. Mean Meline.

The social worker had a kind face. She deftly got rid of Tiffany when she realized she wasn't going to be a comfort to me. She walked me through my options, letting me know that everything in the apartment was mine now. That my parents' lawyer would be taking care of details for me, along with my uncle. That she was only here to get me to British Columbia and that this could happen whenever I liked. Right now, in fact. She had looked into flights. We could fly tonight to join my cousin, who would be arriving in Vancouver the next morning, if that seemed like a good idea. Or I could stay on a few days in Hyannis Port. That I could take anything I liked or decide what I wanted shipped to me later. The rest the executor would arrange to have sold. I looked around the apartment. How did I know what to take into a future I didn't understand?

"Of course, your uncle has a house full of furniture. I have spoken to him. He has a bedroom already furnished for you. But if you'd prefer your own things . . ."

I saw the rocker that I'd squeezed into with my mother for as long as we could both fit. I looked at my bed, just a piece of foam on a small platform. Then I thought of my mother's plate collection. How she'd hunted down Fiestaware. How she said over time it would increase in value. And her grandmother's silver in the drawer. What would she want me to save? Would she still think any of it was important in light of recent developments? All these things that were precious heirlooms. All these things that were here when she no longer was. All these things sheltered, kept safe, to be passed on, our history, I saw how they had no value at all. Everything that my parents had earned money to buy, that seemed so important, now just secondhand junk to be scattered, sold, thrown away. They hadn't marked my parents' place on earth. They hadn't been a parking space or an anchor. Because my parents, when they were gone, were gone.

"I don't want any of it," I said and packed a bag and we left. We walked silently to her car and drove through the rain to the airport. While she bought tickets for us I thought that my father was right. He never talked about growing up. When I asked him questions he would say, "Why? What does it matter? The past is the past. People's lives are in chapters. This is the only chapter I want, this is the chapter I want to last forever and ever, the one with you and your mother." My mother said it was a family quirk. That Jocelyn's father, Uncle Donald, when asked said the same. "Oh, I don't want to talk about that. Haven't we got enough to think about trying to keep our heads above water in the present?"

"Those boys," said my mother, shaking her head. To her, my father and Uncle Donald would always be boys. I wondered if Uncle Marten was a boy, too. I'd never met him. He was the mysterious uncle. The rich uncle. The family iconoclast. The one who never visited. He had been the source of a lot of entertaining speculation around our dinner table on winter nights.

We'd light a candle and put it in the middle of the kitchen table. My father would drink a beer and my mother would knit and they'd tell stories. They both liked to speculate about Uncle Marten.

"Even though he was older than me and Donald, his head was always kind of up in the clouds, so we never expected him to be able to cope with the world at all, let alone get rich," said my father. "We were always a little ashamed of his eccentricities, preferring books to girls or sports or the normal things boys did growing up where we were."

"In a foster home," I said, hoping to prod him into telling me more, but he wouldn't talk about that.

"Some of the time. Marten wasn't going to be a farmer or a fisherman or a pilot like me and Donald. Instead he surprised everyone by breezing through college in record time with several degrees, including an M.B.A. and a Ph.D., and becoming a stockbroker and making a huge amount of money. Then, when he was at the height of his powers and fortune, he quit selling stocks, which he always called a stupid profession, and bought an island off the coast of British Columbia and built a huge Victorian mansion, which none of us have ever seen or are likely to."

But now I would. I'd like to tell my father this. For a long time I thought of things I wanted to tell my father or my mother but couldn't. There was nothing more final than that.

We boarded the plane and flew for a short time, then got on another and flew for a longer time, and as dawn came up got on a third. I looked out the window into early morning nothingness, and the social worker quietly turned the pages of her magazine, as if she must muffle even the noise of that so as not to disturb me. But I wasn't aware of grief so much as of the constant whirring of the plane. And I thought if I could keep that whirring going, I'd never have to be still, and if I never had to be still, none of it could land on me.

My social worker checked us into the hotel in Vancouver. I almost fell asleep in the cab from the airport, but even through my fog I knew the hotel wasn't in a very good part of town. We went into downtown, bright and shining with mountains surrounding the watery edges of the city. The harbor sparkled, people trotted along looking busy, purposeful, alive, healthy, prosperous, right-thinking. Then we left that area and drove east and the buildings became derelict and dingy, and although we were still close to the water the prosperity took a nose-dive. There were bodies in all the doorways: panhandlers, drunks, druggies, homeless. All of them slumped against buildings and doorways. As if legless. The social worker's nostrils swelled and she checked the address on her slip of paper twice when the cabbie pulled up in front of our hotel.

"Oh dear," she said. "I think Marie—that's the social worker escorting your cousin, she made the reservation— she must not know the city very well. I'm afraid she put us all up in a very bad part of town."

I didn't care much at that point; although my room was musty and mildewy, it seemed a minor point, considering, and I fell into a deep sleep and didn't wake up until dinnertime. The plan was to join Jocelyn and Marie for dinner, and then our social workers, their jobs done, would escort us to the helicopter pad where Uncle Marten had a helicopter service that he apparently used all the time. Sam, the pilot, would take us to Uncle's island, Marie explained as we all got back into a cab, deciding to check out and go to dinner with bags rather than return to this neighborhood.

"I'm so sorry," said Marie when we had all seated ourselves self-consciously in the cab. "All the big hotels were full because both the boat show and the marathon are this weekend. The hotel *looked* okay on the Internet. I didn't know how scummy the neighborhood was. You'd think they'd do something about getting those people off the streets. It's a disgrace having to thread your way among them."

"Oh well, never mind, it was only to catch our breaths," said my social worker. Her name never registered with me. The only reason I caught "Marie" was that my social worker was one of those people who have been trained to use people's names in every other sentence until you want to shriek, "Stop it! That doesn't work on me! I see right through it." They never seem to get that it doesn't come off as friendly or kind, just technical.

I tried to smile at Jocelyn, whom I hadn't seen in six years. But she looked at me as if smiling had been a very peculiar thing to have done, and turned her head. I began to wonder if her social worker wore such a pinched expression because she had spent the last few days with Jocelyn. Over dinner Jocelyn said all the right things:

"Please, thank you, yes, I imagine the salmon here would be very good." Even given that the two of us were in a state of shock still, there was a cold collected reserve about her that our parents' deaths didn't account for. It was too practiced to be recent. It was too easy and natural. And, I thought, at a time like this it seemed to serve her well. It was like putting your emotions in an icebox, along with that severed head you told everyone you'd just found lying there. I studied her through dinner, searching for chinks, but could find none. The way she looked at me was the way you are always afraid someone will on those off days when your hair is dirty and your clothes seem particularly tatty and you can't think straight. And there was no giving you the benefit of the doubt. This, her look seemed to say, is who we both know you *really* are. But, of course, she had not expected any better from you, so it needn't ruffle *her* calm. I think it gave the social workers the creeps, and they fell enthusiastically upon each other and spent the rest of the meal talking animatedly, just the two of them, and leaving me to Jocelyn. Which is to say, leaving me to silence.

After dinner we took another cab to the helicopter pad in the harbor, where it seemed to take forever, the four of us standing around in the windy cold, waiting for the helicopter to come to pick up me and Jocelyn. It was odd to have made such an intimate and important journey with another human, a life-changing journey, to be more deeply changed in twenty-four hours than I had been my whole life, and then just to nod goodbye to this witness, no hug or kiss or acknowledgment of a shared experience because, truthfully, there hadn't been one. It had been mine alone. Hers was just a job. It underlined my sudden aloneness, that although people might help me if it was how they earned their living, there was no longer anyone out there who really cared who I was or what happened to me.

I dithered about how to say goodbye in such a situation and was thankful for the chaos of noise and whirling blades. Finally, we were inside the helicopter and waved our goodbyes, Jocelyn's an irritatingly polite and composed white-handed stiff wave, as if she'd been taught at her mother's knee how to wave goodbye to social workers at helicopter pads. My wave was no better. I began it tentatively and took it back several times in indecision, and I could feel the sickly smile on my face as I made it, coming and going the same, but it didn't matter anyway because the social worker had already turned, her head bent toward Marie as they made their way off the pad without looking back.

I tried to distract myself from the view as we flew along, all those lights so far below the seemingly flimsy door, so easy, it seemed to me, to fall out or be *sucked* out by a passing breeze. Before yesterday I would have calmed myself, saying such things never happened, but now I knew such things did happen and sometimes they happened to *you* and there would never be comfort in that thought again.

I wanted to ask Jocelyn what had really happened that night. After all, she had been there. The social worker had given me no details at all. Just that there was some civil unrest in Zimbabwe and there had been a train accident. But I knew it was like putting your tongue on a sore tooth. You knew it was unwise, but you wanted confirmation of what you only suspected. You wanted to know for sure that there was pain there, but then you were sorry that you had. It seemed the height of folly. Then, when your tongue was off, and the throbbing had subsided, you wondered again if the tooth was really sore, so you put out your tongue again. Once, with such a toothache from a cracked tooth, I had done this so often I actually made the crack worse, and the pain was overwhelming until I got to the emergency dentist, and I swore never to do it again. It was better not to know. It was good to have had the tooth experience because I remembered it now and kept my mouth shut. Jocelyn seemed always to keep her mouth shut. I wasn't sure if she knew anything about toothaches. But then, I reasoned, she had the events in Zimbabwe seared in her imagination forever. Or perhaps not. Perhaps she had seen nothing, known nothing, been whisked off in the dead of night, only told about her parents, only told about mine. It was my tongue circling again.

When my parents had informed me that Jocelyn would get to go with her parents to Zimbabwe while I had to stay behind in the company of Tiffany, even though I understood, even though I knew this wasn't a vacation for my parents, that they had musician friends there who were helping them look for property and they were checking out the political climate—that seemed like a bad joke now—I had still been jealous. I knew fairness had nothing to do with anything: Jocelyn's parents could afford to take her, mine could not. And my mom and dad and I would have the rest of our lives in Zimbabwe if we wanted, on our own farm with our own guesthouse if my mother could scout out a property and, with the help of friends there, buy it. So there was no sense being resentful or whiny.

But now I held it against Jocelyn that, as it turned out, the little time remaining to my parents belonged to her and not to me. What did she care about my mother or father? Yet she was the one who got to spend their last days with them. Again, I knew she hadn't done this on purpose, but it felt as if she had grabbed the last piece of cake, eating it alone, when not only was it the last on the plate, but cake had disappeared from the planet and would never be made again. And instead of apologizing for this, or even seeming a little guilty, she sat next to me in the helicopter, dispassionately watching the lights below disappear, unmindful of this transgression, or uncaring, as we crossed the ocean. Half the time on the ride I felt like this, poisonous and full of loathing for her, the other half I felt lucky that whatever there was to see on that horrible night she had seen and I had been spared. That there were some things you never wanted in your memory bank. Seeing the unseeable, the unthinkable, hearing things I didn't want to hear, being pulled away from the bodies I most wanted to stay with, when all my instincts would say to stay, don't leave. I so tortured myself with these two ideas that they consumed me silently for the entire ride, and by the time we got to the house on the island I was staring as blankly and unseeingly as Jocelyn and we must have crossed my uncle's threshold like two zombies. Sam landed the helicopter—an anomaly I didn't at the time appreciate. We took our bags down under the whirring blades and he was off like the social workers, like my whole previous life, without a backward look.

My uncle showed a great deal of immediate sense, I thought at the time, by hardly speaking to us but showing us our rooms and the bathroom and where the extra towels and blankets were and bringing us each a box of cookies and a mug of hot chocolate and then leaving us alone. Later I found out that only the making of the hot chocolate and bringing it to our rooms was uncharacteristic. The rest, what I took to be his sensitivity in remaining quiet and not forcing on us a bunch of sprightly chatter, had nothing to do with deference to our traumatized sensibilities. It was just who he was.

———

Almost immediately I had a closer relationship to the island than I had to either my uncle or my cousin. The island with its wind and waves and pounding rain seemed alive. I wasn't so sure about Uncle Marten or Jocelyn. They were remote in different ways. Jocelyn remained cold and contained and Uncle Marten was never around except at dinner. We ate dinner every night at a long table that sat twenty. I sat at one end, Jocelyn in the middle, and my uncle at the other end. Uncle Marten made the same thing every night, hot dogs and mac and cheese. We ate silently in the drafty dining room with the roar of the fire in the large hearth in the living room, the sound of the ubiquitous wind in the eaves and the rain hitting the windows. Jocelyn cut her hot dogs up with her knife and fork, even the bun, and ate them in tiny, neat pieces. She wiped her mouth on her paper napkin between every bite. My uncle always brought a book down to the table and would read and take notes and then wish us good evening and go to bed. I wasn't sure if he thought that he was being tactful, allowing us the luxury of silence in our grief, or if he regarded us as birds that had accidentally landed in the house and about which he was too distracted to do anything. If Uncle Marten was disturbed by his brothers' deaths he didn't seem to let it interfere with his work. I was surprised then on the third night when he looked up from his book, turned to Jocelyn, and said, "Motoring vacations are all very well, but you can't read in a car. At least, I can't. Nothing worse for motion sickness. That's why I was so pleased when I found out you were taking the train through Zimbabwe. I know Donald said that your mother was afraid of crocodiles."

"Yes," said Jocelyn. "But in the end, it was a waste of time being afraid of crocodiles, wasn't it?"

"Yes, yes, perhaps you're right, well . . . didn't mean to dredge it all up again," he said as if he had mentioned it even once up until then, but perhaps, I thought, he was keeping a tight rein on his desire to talk about it with us, guessing we preferred to be left alone, not to have to think about it if we chose not to. It's so hard to know why anyone really does anything. "Anyhow," he said, rising and putting a marker in his book and shuffling his papers together, "help yourselves to whatever you'd like. I do beg you, whatever you find anywhere. Help yourselves to the um . . ." He looked around the room wildly as if desperate to find something that would tempt us from our sorrows. "Help yourselves to the books!"

There were books in every room. The kitchen was full of shelves of cookbooks and books on food, on the customs of dinner, everything related to the ritual of eating, the gathering, the growing, the hunting of food. Similarly the bathrooms were full of books about water, oceans, sea life, novels like *Moby Dick* and *The Old Man and the Sea* that had nautical themes; *Treasure Island* was there, and *Robinson Crusoe*. Uncle Marten seemed very methodical in this way. The living room and dining room had built-in bookshelves that reached to the high cathedral ceilings. It was impractical if you wanted something from a top shelf, but I guess Uncle Marten had already read those books a long time ago because those shelves were festooned with cobwebs.

All the books on the living room shelves were leatherbound. I asked Uncle Marten where he found so many leatherbound books, and he said he had them customdone, books he liked or, after reading their reviews online in *The New York Times*, thought he *would* like, he ordered and had sent to a bookbinder and bound in leather before being dropped off on the island. It must have cost a fortune. This, more than the size of the house, so large for one person, underscored for me the kind of money Uncle Marten had. It was such an unnecessary thing to do with money. As if you didn't know what to do with the dollar bills that kept piling up.

I came from a house where every dollar was earmarked. Where carrot tops were saved for soup. Where you didn't buy a book you could get from the library. I didn't mind him having so much, why shouldn't he? And why shouldn't he spend it as he liked? But the difference in the way people lived interested me. There was a kind of comfort in the Baggie full of vegetable peelings for soup always in our fridge. It had my mother written all over it. That's a kind of comfort he would never know because he would never have to. There was no need for the security of the soup bag. He could afford to fly in soup from a fine restaurant if that's what he wanted. But it wouldn't be the same. On the other hand, there was probably a kind of comfort for Uncle Marten when another leatherbound book was dropped on the island. That's all those things ever were, comfort, they didn't mean more than that. Like a rug being pulled from beneath us, Jocelyn's and my familiar comforts were gone. I wondered if someday I would regard the arrival of a new leatherbound book with the contentment of continuity. If it would ever be *my* life. Even if it was, it would never be my life as it had been before, believing that all rested solidly in permanence. Not knowing that everything built could be unbuilt in the blink of an eye.

MARTEN KNOCKERS

IT HAD BEEN A LONG TIME since I thought about anyone on earth being connected to me, and so when I heard that my brothers were dead and I was responsible for two girls it hardly seemed possible. Who were they and why would they suddenly be appearing on my doorstep? It was like having cats drop down from the sky along with the rain. It was familiar ordinary things behaving in unexpected ways. They weren't there and then they suddenly were, and none of it made any sense really. I didn't know what to do with living things suddenly *appearing*. Oh well, I thought, I'll just move over and give them a couple of rooms. I had, fortunately, quite a lot of rooms. I hoped they liked books. I had a lot of those, too. I couldn't really think of much else I had to offer them, but perhaps they wouldn't require much. Cats didn't. My roommate in college had a cat, and as I recall all it required was a bit of water and some dry cat food. Of course, I knew better than to give the girls cat food. I didn't mean that literally. And I supposed they would leave me alone to continue working. That was the crucial thing.

As soon as I made my fortune and quit being a stockbroker, I built myself a large Victorian-style mansion and filled it with books because I couldn't wait to go back to what I liked best, reading and studying and *this* time without the kind of nonsense you got at a university. I'd really had enough of all that when I was going for my degrees. You'd think it would be about knowledge at a university, but it isn't. It's about all kinds of other things that are, I suppose, what make up most people's lives. I saw that if I got a university job, my life as a professor would be full of things like acquiring a university wife or, worse, another professor as a spouse, someone who would always tell me I was saying the wrong thing, and having to go to endless parties with other professors and pretend to be interested in their self-interested pursuits and listen to their dull prattle and eat shrimp balls and iffy homemade sushi made by someone in, as I recalled from attending university functions, khakis and Birkenstocks.

You always knew when you were at a party because the professors switched from blue jeans to khakis. As a graduate student I did not have to worry about clothes protocol, but if I became a professor I *would* have to and I was sure I would forget to change into my khakis and arrive in blue jeans and become a social pariah. And *this* is what I would worry about. Not undiscovered knowledge— but pants. I would spend endless hours worried about my pants. I decided I'd rather make a heaping mound of money and worry about what I liked. But I was aware, of course, of the disappointment the family, what was left of it, felt when after what had appeared to be a promising blossoming into respectability and normalcy, I returned to my shameful oddness.

MELINE

UNCLE MARTEN had been a source of endless speculation among the family—our rich, strange relative. The only one of us with any money. Grownups think because they are taller than children their voices carry above their heads, never landing in their ears, but I heard it all, my parents talking about all kinds of things. I heard them when I was supposed to be sleeping and when I was in one room and they were in another or even when I was supposed to be eating and they were drifting about talking from room to room, sure I was too occupied with my food to notice or care about their conversations.

I had only been mildly interested in eavesdropping on my parents' gossip about family members, but now I was glad I had. I was not supposed to have heard my dad telling my mom how Jocelyn's mother thought Uncle Marten had acquired a vulgar amount of money. He said Jocelyn's father thought it wasted on him. My father admitted he was a little jealous and couldn't understand why Marten wouldn't want to help his less fortunate younger brothers, although, naturally, if Marten *had* ever offered him money, he would have returned it in short order. But still, he couldn't help wondering that he didn't even *offer*. It was the lack of the offer that was so curious to him. He knew his brother wasn't stingy. As far as he knew, he didn't hate his family. He hadn't ever even seemed to care about luxury or money. Why then go off alone to some island to sit on all that money like some queer bird on an egg? Who was his brother in the end?

My mother, on the other hand, thought it was lovely that Uncle Marten had so much money. So much money to do with *whatever he liked*. Imagine, Meline! she would say to me while shaking out clean, freshly laundered shirts and smelling them happily. They had just come in off the line on the balcony. She loved folding clothes. *Imagine!* My mother never wanted what other people had. It was like a small burst of exploding light within her all the time, her happy realization of the good things that were. Whether she or someone else had them was never the point for her.

MARTEN KNOCKERS

ONCE I SETTLED into my brand-new completely secluded house, I burned the midnight oil, quite literally sometimes when the power went out, trying to find newness in the world. Trying to find bits and pieces that others hadn't. I have a theory that important things have been left out of the great store of human knowledge and that that is why nothing makes any sense. The great store of human knowledge, after all, is really not so great. What do we really *know*? It's more like a giant jigsaw puzzle with three quarters of the pieces missing from the box. In fact, we're not even sure those pieces are out there anywhere, so when we look, it's really actually pretty futile in a way. That's one way to think about it.

Once when Meline was particularly lucid and wasn't just wandering around with a strange, determined look on her face and lichen in her hair, she asked me what I would think if I found one really good piece of knowledge that made a whole section fit together and make sense. Would I feel I'd done what I'd set out to do with my life? But she didn't get it at all. My dream was to find many,

many pieces. It's why I bought the island, it's why I wanted to live alone in such an isolated way. Because without distractions, and with lots of money and no one I had to kowtow to or be obligated to in order to continue my studies, I could study from day to night and night to day again if I wished, and in such a luxury of time and information without the limits of focus I hoped to find many things.

Most of the discoveries made are not very good and they're made by nincompoops in order to advance their careers, so they're made out by the nincompoops themselves to be of much greater import than they are, and then others get on the bandwagon and build their own nincompoopy schemes and theories from the building blocks of these careerists and nothing of any real importance gets added to the store of human knowledge. Wouldn't it be wonderful to discover something without any desire for personal glory, but just to benefit mankind? Of course, mankind probably didn't care about the motive behind the discovery, did it? It just wanted its soup quick and microwavable. Probably, Meline, I told her, the ancients had microwaves. Lots of information has been lost and needs to be rediscovered. If we could dig up everything they knew . . .

"Who will dig it up—you?" asked Meline.

"Don't be ridiculous. I'm not an archaeologist. No, anything I discover will be new. Maybe it will be lost knowledge rediscovered, but that comes to the same thing. Anyway, the point is to have as much knowledge as possible."

"And do what with it?" Meline asked.

I just shook my head. I do feel that if you don't already understand scholarship for scholarship's sake there is no point trying to explain it to you. You should take up another hobby. You should knit.

Twice a year I would leave the island for academic conferences. There I would give papers and so get a chance to share what I had found. Disappointingly, my papers always seemed to be better than everyone else's. I realized that I had the luxury of time to do only my research. I didn't have to teach as well. But even so, I would think the other presenters would occasionally come up with *something* better than they did. I always held out hope that I would meet interesting people and not come back to the island confirmed in the mediocrity of academics. But time and time again, I'd arrive home thinking that anyone who has chosen academia has to be too stupid to find his mouth with his fork.

After the last trip I slammed my briefcase onto the table and stormed to bed. Conferences invariably put me in a bad mood. I went so full of expectation, I imagined some kind of idyllic community of scholars sitting together, sharing our enthusiasm, piecing our knowledge into some kind of great quilt, but then I would simply get lost in the muddle of people, the universities and conference centers, the hotels and dinners and cocktail parties and speaking with professors. All those people looking at me funny, thinking I was some kind of mad genius, a Howard Hughes character. And then I got the letters. People wanting money to fund projects, fund careers, fund themselves, fund travel. "Fund off," I would think to myself, ripping them into shreds.

One professor, wanting research money, buttonholed me at a cocktail party, praising my paper extravagantly. "And you don't even have expertise in this area," she gushed.

"I live on an island, madame," I said. "I have a lot of time to think."

People were, by and large, exasperating.

And now, although my two young nieces behaved very well, I hadn't a clue what to do with them. Even though, between my work and their grief, we hardly saw each other. Of course, I was very upset about the loss of my brothers and I realized that the girls must be even more upset about the loss of their fathers and mothers, but collective mourning is not my style. You do not move to an island if you are fond of group activities. I felt badly, though, really dreadful about what I could only guess they were going through. But beyond that I really did not know what to do for them. And I was ashamed that I did not enjoy having dinner with them, especially because it was the only time I spent with them, if you could call sitting at the same table and reading while eating spending time, which I did because it was certainly more time than I had spent with anyone else in the last twenty years or so. Really, by my standards we were becoming quite intimate.

Finally, after a week, my conscience smote me even about this. I realized it was not a worthy thing to do, to shun my responsibility for their care even to avoiding dinner conversation. That, despite myself, if I was going to take on this newfound responsibility I would have to change. Or at least amend some of my habits. My heartfelt belief was that all meals should be eaten hunched over a desk with your nose in a book and everything you were eating chopped up and eaten out of a bowl with a spoon, the better to scoop it up without having to lift your eyes from the page. I continued to eat breakfast and lunch this way but stopped reading at dinner, although I still brought a book and notebook and pen down with me, hopeful that Meline and Jocelyn would be somehow uninterested in me and I would be granted a reprieve from all this noxious stimulation.

The second fact I had to face about the dinners was that my nieces didn't seem to be enjoying their hot dogs and mac and cheese. Not even when I tried to enliven things by topping the hot dogs with Cheez Whiz. They ate stolidly, uncomplainingly, but occasionally wincing, and I felt ashamed and furtive and muttered things like, "I know I read about this in a magazine somewhere. At least I think I did. What did they call it? Dogs topped with cheese? No, that wasn't it. Sunny dogs! Yes, I think that was the rather perky name for it. Sunny dogs. You put Cheez Whiz on the dogs, the sun so to speak, you see. Oh well," I said softly, feeling defeated. "Oh well."

Jocelyn and Meline startled every time I spoke. Then they dropped their eyes, apparently as embarrassed as I was by the hole I was digging for myself.

Worst of all, instead of thinking about the missing element in the unified field theory, I found myself thinking about the food situation the rest of the night. I wasn't used to defeat or to behaving in ways of which I was ashamed or making up stories about reading recipes in magazines. I knew I must amend this immediately and stop making embarrassing gestures to cover up my lethargy about food. Perhaps I ought to start eating better myself. I didn't keep up with health issues. I wasn't as young as I used to be. I'd already lost my hair. Most of it anyway, except for two rows at the sides of my head. If I wasn't going to learn to plan meals and cook, perhaps it was time to let someone else worry about the food. After all, even I knew that hot dogs and mac and cheese were not acceptable dinner fare for all. It was never, not once, served at any of the fancy conference dinners I went to, it wasn't even served at the less fancy rubber chicken dinners. In fact, to be perfectly honest, I'd never seen it served anywhere at all. Not even on planes.

I had gotten the idea from the television one night in a hotel room at a conference in Manitoba when I'd seen a

Kraft commercial and a happy mom, a happy suburban *Canadian* mom, who was somehow even *blander*, safer, and more reliable than a happy suburban *American* mom, putting a plate of macaroni and cheese and hot dogs in front of her three tow-haired little boys, and the boys' sheer delight in being served such cheerful suburban bland Canadian food and the mom's pleasure in being able to provide the kind of food that would make her otherwise rather lifeless little brood brim over with excitement. It was so much happiness spilling over everywhere, so much undeserved, mindless contentment from so simple a thing, it was so easy for them, there were no dark skeletons there, here were lives so simple that a plateful of bland foodstuffs initiated an attack of sheer rapture, and I'd thought, yes, that looks easy enough. I can do that. I have not sunk so low into the depths of human despair, the deep endless well of the dark night of the soul, that I cannot be salvaged by a little mac and cheese. I can be my own woman of the house and serve such things to myself. Perhaps to be bland is to be good. Perhaps we are saved not by our passion, our pain, or our search but by our utter indifference to any of that nonsense. Perhaps it is not truth and the struggle to find it but really blandness that will set us free. Perhaps I should join their lifeless but utterly contented party. At least, when all's said and done, with a case of mac and cheese and a freezer full of hot dogs, I will never have to cook.

This had come on the depressing heels of a talk one of

my fellow conferencers had had with me at another interminable cocktail party when she was trying to convince me in a coquettish way that what I needed was a woman to share the island with. I had mistakenly told her I lived alone there, and she had picked up the ball and run, in my consideration, sadly afoul with it. A woman to iron my shirts, she'd said, pointedly staring at what peeked out from beneath my wool sports coat, for I like cotton shirts and I don't know how to iron or want to learn and have always figured shirts aren't really visible under a jacket and tie anyway, so I arrived everywhere sadly wrinkled. Since most of my fellow academics are similarly wrinkled, perhaps not so badly, but certainly not crisp and polished, I never felt particularly noticeable until this woman suggested that I'd be less wrinkled if I married. I bought drip-dry shirts after that. I didn't like them as well, they weren't as comfortable, but they didn't invite comment. Then she said I must have someone to cook for me, too.

"You women!" I sputtered indignantly. "You spend half the time at conferences banding together and sharing information about chilly climates. How you're done out of your due at your place of work, how the men still say 'he' when they should say 'he or she' and on and on, and then when it comes to the cocktail party you get drunk and revert to something your mothers would be ashamed of, telling someone that he needs someone to cook for him. Well, I am astounded. Astounded and astonished.

Astonished and astounded!" And then I temporarily forgot her altogether as I pondered the difference between astonishment and astoundedment. Astonished was perhaps just surprised while astounded implied some kind of moral judgment attached. A disapproving version of astonished. You could be happily astonished but could you be happily astounded? I didn't think so.

This little outburst, as you can imagine, even if I hadn't drifted off in thought as if the woman simply weren't there, had cut the conversation short or, at any rate, shorter. This new tack in the conversation had left her breathless and appalled but it had upset me far more. I didn't exactly panic, but it did cause me a certain amount of unease. I did not want to become like those people who were found dead under twenty years' worth of old newspapers. I did not want to start collecting cats and then slide down the slippery slope of just opening another tin of cat food for myself in the evening. I didn't feel better until I saw the Kraft commercial and realized here was a meal I could make and eat, to be as nurtured and nurturing as the tow-headed brood and their no doubt overly involved mother. And that, menu wise, was that.

But now I knew my perfect menu would no longer do. If I was going to be a good guardian and a good host I was going to have to do better. This stressed me. It meant I was going to have to think about something that I had no interest in, that wasn't profitable to me or my studies. But I did it anyway and that was how I came up with

Mrs. Mendelbaum. That is, I came up with the happy thought that I had the money to hire people to think about things for me that I didn't want to think about myself. That I needn't have food on my brain if there was someone else around who did. A cook was the answer.

The night I was writing the advertisement for the cook, I heard Jocelyn sneezing over and over. She may have been sneezing repeatedly before then, perhaps I only tuned into it now as I tuned into their need for a more varied diet. At any rate Jocelyn confessed, when prodded, that she was terribly allergic to dust. That was when I noticed the dust bunnies everywhere, the cobwebs hanging from the ceiling, the dirt on all the floors. When Meline screamed "MOUSE" from the bathroom, I realized something would have to be done about that, too. Until then I had let the mice have their way. They seemed to want to come in in the late fall when it was growing cold outside, and at first I had found this very annoying. I didn't want to share my space with any living creature, and mice were noisy in their own way, but dealing with them required more energy and ingenuity than I had, so I simply set traps in my bedroom and the kitchen and let them have the rest of the house. After all, it was a big house, room for all. Most of the time I forgot to empty the traps. I really was the most deplorable housekeeper no matter how you looked at it. And for some reason all the drains in the house backed up, particularly after a hard rain. I looked at the kitchen sink, with six inches of backed-up water in it, and thought, What is one supposed to *do*? So I amended the ad I was writing from cook to cook/housekeeper—some rodent control required; and the first one to answer the ad was Mrs. Mendelbaum.

MRS. MENDELBAUM

EVERYONE HAD DIED. All of them. Ganz kaput. Now I needed the money and something, I think, else. What else I am not sure, so I answer the ad to find out. Either find out or take care of it without finding out. Does it matter? The helicopter leaves me there alone looking at it. It all sparkles, the ocean, so many windows in that big house. What did I know, then? I thought this Marten Knockers would be some alter kucker in a condominium. Did I think he would be living alone in such a big place? How should I know such things? I had never answered an ad before. Cooking or cleaning I had done, yes, for my own family. For my husband and four sons. Now all dead. A person with maybe not such big expectations I could cook or clean for. But this? Who knows what such a person living all alone in such luxury would expect. A g'vir. Gut far him! He should eat so well with some fancy-shmancy cook.

This is my adventure. My first adventure alone. Without Ansel, what did I care how it turned out? Still, such a big house, it was not feeling so much like my little adventure. It was feeling like maybe my little fraud. But oh well, I should worry, probably he wouldn't hire me anyway. Probably I would not be here after the interview. Er zol vaksen vi a tsibeleh, mit dem kop in drerd; ich hob es in drerd. He's probably looking for some hotsie-totsie girl living here all alone.

Then, so fast he hires me. Does he ask me questions? No. Does he ask to see references? No. He tells me he has no interest in such things and he wants to be done with it, so he hires me. Like that. A man should take some trouble unless, of course, he doesn't care who he hires because he wants not just a hotsie-totsie girl but to get out his ax! Such an isolated place. So easy to bury them on this farkuckt island. Perhaps, *perhaps I am not the first!* Who else would live so alone? A butcher knife I keep by my bed after that. But no, meshugeh he turns out to be, but not in that way.

After that I call my friend Sophie Babilinska, who lives across the hall from me, that she should send my things with this helicopter pilot Sam. And to tell the landlord my apartment can be let. Sophie warns me, a crazy thing, she says, an impetuous thing, moving to this island when I know so little about my employer. I think, of course, Sophie may be right, but ech I say and turn deaf ears. "I haf a new beginning in my life and we should all haf that. After all, what do I have left, Sophie? Shmek tabik."

"Your husband is rolling in his grave, mark my words, Zisel," says Sophie.

"He should roll in his grave when he didn't roll in his life? Trust me, a roller he wasn't. I have work to do. I cannot think of the past. I have eleven bedrooms to keep clean."

"And who is this alter kucker? What kind of a house has eleven bedrooms?" asks Sophie.

"A rich man's. What do you think? Just send my things."

"Why don't you come back for them yourself, then?" asks Sophie.

"My new employer needs my services immediately," I say. This sounds good, I think, but I think, too, it is not right that he should demand I immediately cook and clean and not leave the island. I do not know that he is only thinking to himself, he wants nothing to do with such business, he has hired me to cook and clean, let me start cooking and cleaning. Yes, a butcher's knife next to the bed.

"Your services, oy vey, I shouldn't ask," says Sophie, who is Polish but speaks German, Yiddish, and English, too. I take her to the Jewish Community Center with me on Fridays to help make the challahs. Sophie is good with bread.

"Get your mind out of the gutter, Sophie," I say. "Es past nit. Who would want us at our age in such a way?"

"Believe me, plenty," says Sophie. "There are some men, even dead they want you."

"In your dreams," I say. I have been in Canada for many years, so a few expressions I know. But still I think in other times, in other languages. I exist sometimes, I think, here, sometimes in the past, the time, for me always, of my heart. It was as Ansel said to me when he died, these days are not our days, when we had our boys, growing up, that was the meat of our life. Now dinner is over, not even dessert to look forward to, all finished. What is between now and nightfall? And here on this farkuckt strange island, no TV, no shopping, no movies, where we cannot see others living their lives, no connection to other people, always before I have lived among many people, like drops of water in a big wave. Here, there is just us. Everyone extinguished, kaput, everyone we had loved, our pasts, gone. Who would have thought you could spend your life collecting people to have them all gone, to be again completely alone? Who tells you it will be this way? Who should know?

"He could be one of *them*," said Sophie. Sophie believes Nazis are in big homes in Canada. Made rich by stealing from the Jews. She does not even dare say "Nazis" but whispers "them" in case they are listening.

"Sophie, you see Nazis everywhere. They're dead. All of them. All the Nazis, all their victims, the whole business kaput," I say to her.

"Some things are never kaput," says Sophie and hangs up.

And so my things come and I meet these two girls, these wisps who do not even make noise. Who barely notice my coming. Who have been so quiet I did not know they were here. So I make dinner from what I can find, which isn't much, let me tell you. A freezer full of hot dogs! So many boxes of mac and cheese! Enough already. I have that tsedrait helicopter pilot deliver some meat, some potatoes, some carrots. No more hot dogs for you, Mr. Fancy Pants, I say to myself as I cook. Then they eat.

"Thank God," says Mr. Knockers, "I can get back to work."

"Thank God," say the girls.

"Thank Got," I say for reasons of my own.

JOCELYN

AT THE FIRST Mrs. Mendelbaum–made meal, Uncle Marten pointed to his plate and asked, "What's this? It's brown. It seems somehow browner than most foods. It's awfully brown for a food. Are some foods browner than others? Is it a meat? It is. It *is* a meat, by God." He was poking it with his fork in a curious, detached way that my mother wouldn't have approved of. My mother was British and had brought me up the way she had been brought up. My mother taught my father table manners as well because she said his had been sketchy when she married him. I never noticed because by the time I was old enough to notice, my mother had his under control. But sometimes she talked to me about it. The manners he had when she first met him. And how she had had to work a miracle to get him to even sit up straight at table. But now he did, back straight, feet flat on the floor, napkin on lap, no dilly-dallying. Eat your food in a businesslike way, wipe smudges off your mouth with the corner of your napkin, don't drink or talk with your mouth full, take small, tasteful bites, say please and thank you, ask for things to be passed, no elbows, no rude noises, no mention of what one was eating, all conversation should be impersonal, anecdotal, and of interest to all, and always, always remember that Britain is better than Canada and much, *much* better than the United States of America, where restaurant portions are too big, people talk too loudly and too much and at inappropriate times, and all the inhabitants wear white shoes.

"What is this fascination with white shoes that they have? And gym shorts and gym shoes and little white socks when they go out? If they're so obsessed with the gym, why are they all so fat?" my mother said to me and variations on the theme. By the time I was nine I was suspicious of Canadians and absolutely terrified of Americans. Their influence was pandemic. My mother said if it wasn't for the Americans, Britain would still have red phone booths. She seemed to find the passing of the red phone booth a particularly worrisome sign, as well as the destruction of hedgerows and the building of that big monstrous Ferris wheel that ruined the London skyline. As if it were no longer necessary to take England seriously, she said scoldingly, as if it were now all one big theme park.

I looked down the table at Meline. She was sitting on one of her feet, twirling her hair between her fingers and occasionally putting her finger experimentally into her potatoes. I suppose that's just another thing that Americans do. I watched Meline to find out what other quirks Americans had that my mother hadn't had time to tell me about.

"The meat is brisket," I said briskly, answering Uncle Marten's question about the brown meat. I knew that I didn't have my mother's British accent, but I had her inflections, more British than Canadian, and I chopped my words out more precisely than the rest of them. It's a form of respect, really, not to drag your speech on and on as if everyone wants to hear the sound of your voice. "And the potatoes are kugel. It's a kind of pudding. I ran into Mrs. Mendelbaum before dinner and she gave me the menu."

"Well, imagine that!" said Uncle Marten, snorting indignantly. "She did not give *me* the menu. Oughtn't she to have given *me* the menu? Never mind, on second thought, I'd much rather not know."

"This is supposed to be *pudding*?" asked Meline skeptically. "This isn't pudding. Someone is going to have to explain to Mrs. Mendelbaum what pudding is. This is more like hash browns or scalloped potatoes or something. But it isn't pudding. Maybe you didn't understand. Her English isn't that good. Maybe she said something else."

"Like what?" I asked.

"Like 'budding.' Maybe in German hash browns are called budding."

"It isn't supposed to be a *sweet* pudding. It's a savory pudding," I said, cutting myself another tiny bite of brisket and popping it into my mouth and wondering when this interminable meal would be over.

"*Savory?*" Meline said. "As in 'to savor'? I don't think anyone is going to savor the idea of some potatoes masquerading as pudding and coming along on the plate next to the meat when anyone could tell you a pudding is supposed to be served at the end of the meal. And sweet."

"Well said," said Uncle Marten, tapping on his wineglass with his butter knife for emphasis. It rang nicely and he did it several more times, apparently enjoying it and looking abstracted. Then he rang his water glass. Then he got up and went to the china cupboard muttering something about looking for a tumbler that was made of plain glass rather than crystal. Meline and I watched him bemused. It was like living with an impulsive two-year-old.

"As in 'not sweet,' " I said. I really didn't care what they thought of savories because their opinions were, I was sure, beneath my concern. I was sure my mother would regard them the way she did the women in her quilting society who used paper napkins. "Didn't your mother ever serve you a savory?"

"I don't know anyone who has ever served a savory, or, at any rate, called it that," said Uncle Marten, back at his seat and eating his brisket with gusto now. He explained to us about some family of tow-headed boys in a commercial. That he could even see the Kraft commercial mom serving it to her witless but (he had since decided) secretly evil brood. The very blandness of those blond-headed boys, with their milky skin and snub noses, their uniform bland expressions of delight at dinner, haunted him. He had been brooding about them for weeks and he began to see their blandness as a mask, covering up their true natures, for who could really be so bland? No, they were demons in his daymares, devils smiling for the camera and then going out nights to perform ritual sacrifices. By now, he admitted, he was terrified of them and, whenever they surfaced in his thoughts, tried to put them immediately back out. Was he *serious*?

"Your mother was extraordinary, dear. I could tell from her Christmas cards. She really believed in all this nonsense, I think, about savories and dry sherry and all that British stuff that everyone else back there in Britain threw away with the dinosaurs. She really seemed to think that the preservation of such things would save the world. Well, bless her, bless anyone I say who thinks they have a formula for saving the world." He muttered this last to himself, examining a little bowl full of purple sauce that he apparently hadn't noticed before.

"Beet horseradish," I said, smiling politely but mentally rolling my eyes. Canadians were turning out just as my mother had warned me. I must redouble my guard.

I grew up on a thousand acres in Saskatchewan where my father was a crop duster and my mother oversaw the farm. I was homeschooled and seldom met anyone but the farm workers and an occasional Canadian guest whom my mother had approved. But it took so much to approve one of these, with such a powerful nationality strike against him to begin with, that they were few and far between. Mostly we had other Britons visiting us because my mother belonged to a traveling aid society for visiting Britons. She put people up for a reasonable rate in the guest cottage she had made my father build in his practically nonexistent spare time. My mother had no spare time either and she had no sympathy for anyone else having or wanting any. The society preapproved all its members in advance, of course. When my mother filled out the application to be a member herself and was asked what kind of people she would not be comfortable housing she had typed in, "We don't want any serial killers. Or those of a criminally bent nature. No one who snores. And of course no Americans." She knew we could not hear a snorer from the guest cottage, but she disapproved of snorers on principle. To her they represented a sound sleeper, and a sound sleeper was someone who enjoyed his sleep a little too much and was therefore apt to be lax in his other personal habits as well. One should sleep lightly, she said, if at all.

It was because my mother was a member of this society that she and my father and Meline's father and mother and I were traveling through Zimbabwe. We could not have afforded to go otherwise. It wasn't that I blamed the society, but I couldn't help thinking of them as one of the reasons it happened.

It had been my mother's dream to return someday to England, although she knew it would be difficult to get my father to leave the prairies and the unbroken line of land to sky and the miles of airspace to traverse and the acres of crops to dust. There are so few things to really love in this world, he said to me, the only time he ever brought up my mother's desire to return to England and her tiny campaign in that direction, that the things that you find to love you should hang on to forever because time is short and you have to spend it, as much as you can, with your heart engaged. But back then I didn't know what this meant. Time seemed endless to me, to stretch to the horizon and beyond, an unbroken line like the prairies, and I didn't feel the need to hang on to things. And my mother had already instructed me on the care of my heart, and although I didn't understand my mother's advice any more than my father's, I took it in as

I did all things pertaining to my mother, as the *right way.*
What did my father mean now by saying you engaged
your heart? My mother told me that things happened to
you and they acted *upon* your heart. You had no choice in
the matter. And you saw things differently accordingly.
Wasn't that what life *was?* So you protected your heart,
that fragile, beating, bloody mass of meat, as soon as you
learned how easily things from the outside could damage
it. *That's* what life was: a gauntlet of events battering you,
and you tried to slip through as unbroken as possible.
You crouched around your heart the way a mother
crouches around her child under sniper fire, protecting
him from bullets. Doing what she can. All your energy,
according to my mother, had best go into protection and
preservation. The idea of engaging your heart, going out
to the front line, so to speak, was alien to her.

I didn't even give it any thought, what I loved and
what I didn't. I assumed the only life I would have was
the one that had been handed to me. The idea of making
a life, starting from scratch, being responsible for what
was to be, was foreign. My days were the endless days of
the farm, the sounds, the farm sounds, the lowing cows,
the birds when I awoke, the wind rushing through long
grasses, the sound of combines, reapers, tractors, the
whirr of machinery, and the silence evenings. The
sights: the lovely swaying motion of things, grasses, laundry, my mother's quiet solid movements, never resting,

never stopping, the rhythm of the world, my mother's rhythm, unquestioningly, always. Not until Zimbabwe did I even guess that there were other rhythms, other days, other ways to be. But then I had never lost anyone and didn't know that when you lost someone, you disappear with that person, the part of you that fit with them, leaving you wondering who you are. That though you can remember that person and yourself, the self you were with that person is gone.

My mother and father had not seen eye to eye on Canada and Canadians and so they didn't discuss it. And because my mother couldn't discuss it with my father, but it preyed upon her mind, she discussed it frequently with me. My mother was homesick and she thought Canada was a barbarous country where people did things the wrong way. I was afraid to leave our farm without her; I thought I needed always to be with someone who at least knew the right way to do things, to insulate me from all those people doing things wrong. She said we didn't belong in Canada. Now that I was here on the island, it was a comfort to remember the things my mother had told me. To know that the strangeness and unease I felt with these people was in part because I did not belong with them. My mother had been right. People were not following the rules of civilized society. They were being strange, North American, unruly, wrong. And they poked at their food like animals.

MELINE

"AND YOU, MY DEAR," said Uncle Marten, looking down the length of the table at me, "should try this very brown meat. It's really rather good. I know it looks like a big mess. Really, as if someone had thrown up on your plate, but it's tasty and probably nutritious. Yes, I think Mrs. Mendelbaum will work out fine."

I took a bite. It wasn't just that I had never eaten meat before coming to the island, although I didn't tell anyone there that. I had liked the hot dogs okay, just not every night, and besides hot dogs were familiar because I had eaten tofu dogs, which were in the same ballpark taste-wise. But the brisket flavor was dark and deep and complicated, and because my mother never used salt in her cooking, the sheer saltiness was overwhelming. I put down the rest of my forkful. "I think it's crap," I said. I think I said this partly because I knew it would make Jocelyn wince, and it did. It annoyed me that she could continue so primly, so distantly in the face of something so disastrous it should have broken down any barriers between us, but we went our separate ways during the day, meeting up only at meals, and apparently nothing ruffled her calm.

"Oh no, surely not?" asked Uncle Marten. He looked

terrified at the thought that Mrs. Mendelbaum might not work out after all and this, of course, had not been my intention. I almost relented enough to eat the rest of the brisket just to put him at ease, but I couldn't. I knew it would make me sick. Besides, I didn't want that kind of power. I didn't want to feel that menus would be arranged around what I liked or didn't like. I didn't want to have to worry all the time about whether I could eat something and what hung in the balance if I didn't.

MARTEN KNOCKERS

I REGARDED MELINE with furrowed brow. If she did not like Mrs. Mendelbaum's cooking, or Mrs. Mendelbaum was going to go off on strange cooking tangents involving overly brown meat, then the whole damn thing would have to start again. The advertising, the interviewing . . . but no, I realized with sudden relief, *this* time, if Mrs. Mendelbaum had to leave because the girls could not eat what she cooked, I could quite fairly put *them* in charge of hiring the next cook. *They* could advertise. *They* could interview. I would be out of it altogether. And that way it didn't matter if Mrs. Mendelbaum worked out or not. It wouldn't impinge on me. I finished my dinner serenely after that, even making small happy eating noises.

Later that night, up in my room, I wondered for a second if I should have encouraged Meline to try a second bite of brisket, whether she wanted to or not. Weren't you supposed to encourage children to expand their horizons? That was the whole problem, I didn't know how to be with anyone, but at least I'd never been put in *charge* of anyone before; it hadn't mattered if I didn't know what to do with them. But now here I was ostensibly in charge and I didn't have a clue what to do with those girls. Surely young women this age were beyond the need of encouragement. That is, I didn't have to encourage them to be any particular way, they had their own ideas at this point, did they not? They were nothing more than small adults really, weren't they? Just needing some feeding and housing until they went off to college. That seemed reasonable, a job I could perform with some confidence. I wasn't expected really to *mold* them in any way, was I? I, myself, at such an age, well, at any age really, would have been highly offended at the idea of anyone molding *me*. It would have been an insufferable liberty. I would never inflict that on others. Not to mention that I really didn't care or know how.

For a terrible second I had visions of my nieces as clay and myself back in grade-seven art class with a lump of the shapeless messy useless stuff in front of me and the teacher telling me I must do something original. So I made something shapeless and labeled it "molecular nuclei." No, no, said the teacher, throwing it in the bin to be recycled. Something original but recognizable. So I made a dog with six legs. "No, no," said the teacher. Everyone else in class had progressed to mosaics. Something original, recognizable, and plausible. Well, this had stumped me. Surely art, real art, was not pinioned by all these criteria. And surely they couldn't expect everyone to be an artist. Why, probably nobody in the whole school, the whole town was a real artist. How many real artists were born in a single century, let alone in one school? Oh, certainly there were lots of clever people and lots of clever people making money in their clever artistic ways. But real artists, like real geniuses, were few and far between, so this time, I picked up my lump of clay and threw it in the recycling and took an F for the course. I cannot mold. My brothers, when making me guardian, should have taken this into consideration. I was not an artist and I couldn't mold. I could pay bills. It would have to do.

MELINE

I ATE THE POTATO KUGEL, which was not too far from the kind of vegetarian casseroles my mother put together in our apartment over the store in Hyannis Port. My mother was a marimba player and had lived in Zimbabwe when she was younger. Her dream was to settle there, where twenty thousand dollars would buy you acres of land and a house. She planned to run a guesthouse, not unlike the kind that Jocelyn's mother ran on their farm, only open to everyone and especially, she hoped, visiting musicians like herself, without much money, visiting vegetarian musicians who had respect for the land and for all people and wanted only peace and music and harmony. She had friends in Zimbabwe who said they could help. It was odd, I thought, that in pursuing this she had died in some horrible way. Anyway, I imagined it was a horrible way. I spent a lot of time blocking the images of the ways you could die in a train wreck. All the mangled ways. They were none of them peaceful or harmonious.

My father had a small chartered plane business. Most of the profits he made went back into the business, so my mother said that they could never afford the land they would like in the United States. Zimbabwe was the hope. She didn't want an acre or two, she wanted land as far as her eye could see. She wanted something wild. I think she would have liked the island, although it might have been too cold and rainy for her. She liked the heat. She loved summers when the apartment, which remained un-air-conditioned, grew sweltering. The hotter it was, the more energetic she felt, unlike my father and me, who would go down to the beach in the evenings and try to stay there until it had cooled enough to be bearable in our bed-rooms.

I was always aware that we were poor and that everyone else in Hyannis Port was rich. It wasn't the truth probably, but the rich seemed to glow in their brightly colored clothes. The rich in Hyannis Port wore lime green and bright yellow and gleaming white ankle socks and sneakers of an unassailable whiteness as though their wearers walked on air. Slightly above the ground. As if their money allowed them the luxury of never having to touch the pavement. My mother in her long cotton India print dresses stood out. She dressed me in similar India print clothes until I was old enough to object. Then she got my clothes from the thrift store and I wore the faded cast-offs of the lime-green-alligator-on-the-pocket people. I wasn't concerned about fitting in, but I didn't want to look as if my clothes were making a statement either, as if I were overly proud of being poor or thumbing my nose at their wealth. My mother didn't care one way or the other. She felt she fit in fine with them and their pert trim neat haircuts and the healthy whites of their eyes as if they'd been fed the premium brand of pet food.

At school everyone liked to pretend they knew the Kennedys and, when the summer tourists arrived, pretend to *be* the Kennedys. I didn't care for the Kennedys. It seemed to me too often people confused virtue with believing in them. People were superstitious about virtue. As if, if you believed in the right things loudly enough, you became part of a club of people whom nothing bad happened to. But my mother was apolitical. Once a canvassing Democrat had steeled her courage and knocked upstairs on our recessed front door. She must have needed every vote to bother—it never looked like anyone lived there. When my mother said she didn't plan to vote the woman told her that if she was not part of the solution she was part of the problem, and my mother said that, on the contrary, some people weren't part of the solution or the problem, they just wanted to play music.

That was what I liked best about my mother. She always spoke her mind. Not in an unpleasant way. Just in an unafraid way. It seemed to me she lived her whole life in an unafraid way, which was why it seemed so unfair that her life was cut short. Would she have lived longer if she'd been afraid? Would this have kept her from going to Zimbabwe or believing she could have a guesthouse there? Or would her short life have been just more unhappy? Clouded by fear. It bothered me more than anything else that I would never know if things would have turned out differently if we could, for instance, have gotten back my parents' lives and done them over, fixed the fatal flaws that caused them to end up on that train, riding, riding to whatever bloody, unvegetarian place they had arrived.

I wanted to be like my mother, light and open and full of graceful courage, but I think I was more like my dad, who was forthright and stand-up but also enjoyed giving someone a good poke now and then. Well, we were none of us perfect. Not even my mother, who had her own small vices. She couldn't make chocolate chip cookies without eating the entire batch. My father would come home saying the apartment smells great, what have you been making, and my mother would look around furtively and say . . . cookies . . . finally because although she was a pig when it came to cookies, she was not a liar, and my father would say, oh, fantastic, where are they, and my mother would say, none left, in a businesslike manner that hoped to cut short any further speculation about the fate of the cookies, and start to play the marimba really loud. My mother always wanted to lose ten pounds, but she never seemed to figure out that a good start would be to stop making cookies. She said, I am going to make cookies, Meline, and I am only going to eat one. It would be me who would only get one, at most two, then she'd tell me no more, they weren't good for me, and when I came in the kitchen later a terrible look would be in her eye, like a cornered fox, and I'd know the cookies had once again gotten the best of her.

In the end she came to believe that the cookies were evil. It was the only time I ever heard her call anything evil. As a rule she didn't believe in evil, but it was the only way she could account for the cookies' sway.

One day I came home from school and tried to help her overcome her struggle with the cookies with a saying my teacher had written on the board that morning: ALWAYS PADDLE YOUR OWN CANOE, by which I thought she could extrapolate Don't let the cookies control you. My mother sat down and thought about that, but she didn't seem to get the implication. "The one I like is DON'T BE FURIOUS,

BE CURIOUS," she said, pouring us each a glass of lemonade. I thought we were going to segue into an examinatory chat about such things, but instead she just looked off into space and sipped her lemonade and said, "Do you think that cat next door was really spayed? It looks pregnant to me."

I tried to think of a favorite aphorism of my father's, but all I could recall him giving me in the way of organized advice was "DON'T TAKE ANY CRAP FROM ANYBODY." It's not exactly something you'd want needlepointed on a pillow.

Still, I had thought, a judicious blend of this advice would probably see me through. I had thought this on Monday still. By Tuesday I had changed my mind. Wednesday I was clinging to them again. Today I wasn't sure. Tomorrow it would probably be something else. Maybe not. I took another bite of kugel. My world was gone. My world was gone.

"Kugel? Brisket?" I said to Jocelyn. "I never even *heard* those words before."

MARTEN KNOCKERS

JOCELYN SAID, "Mrs. Mendelbaum told me that it was what she used to cook for her family. She said she cooked good simple food, nothing fancy. She isn't a professional cook, you know. Or a professional housekeeper. She took the job because she couldn't stand listening to only her own sounds every day in her apartment. It creeped her out. I'm paraphrasing, of course. She wanted to be someplace where there were other people's sounds. You knew when you hired her that she was awfully old, didn't you, Uncle Marten?"

"I did *not*!" I said. Who thought about such things? "She doesn't look it." There was a pause as I considered this. "*You* don't think she looks old, do you?"

"Didn't it say her age on her résumé?" asked Jocelyn, ignoring my question and continuing to calmly cut her meat into teeny, tiny bits.

"Her what? Oh yes. Those things. Well, I didn't ask for one."

"References?" asked Jocelyn.

"No, of course not. Well, I mean she *looks* okay, doesn't she? Not like an ax murderer or anything. And, after all, if someone wants to make up a résumé and references, that's easy enough to do."

"Yes, but you can phone the references to check them out," said Jocelyn. "That's what they're there for. You can find out if someone is really too old to be working."

I felt cornered and bored. It was all much ado about nothing if you asked me. "Yes, well, I suppose you can. But there's nothing to stop people from having their friends pretend to be phony references. Face it, Jocelyn, my dear, if someone in your future employ wants to hoodwink you, well, they can. So you may as well just dispose of the whole nonsense."

"Or go with your gut," Meline said, shoving rolls into her mouth. She had apparently given up on dinner and made rolls the main course.

"Exactly," I said, looking at Meline gratefully. "Go with your gut. My gut says she looks perfectly okay." I pulled my glasses down to the tip of my nose and glanced over them in the direction of the kitchen where Mrs. Mendelbaum was putting the finishing touches on a honey cake. "She looks completely capable of doing whatever a younger cook could do. Heavy lifting and such."

"Heavy lifting?" Meline asked, laughing and spraying crumbs everywhere. Jocelyn looked politely away.

"Yes, in the kitchen. Heaving pots of pasta water or heavy roasts and turkeys about," I said imperturbably, returning to my meal. Girls were really very silly. Anyone could see the woman could cook and that's what I hired her for, so what was all this talk of résumés and references? I wasn't hiring for NASA, after all. And how the heck was I supposed to know if someone was too old to work unless they told me so? I could rarely remember how old I myself was. The only important thing about people was their ideas, and the tragedy was that they seldom had any. "I don't even know how old *you* are," I said, continuing aloud my train of thought.

"I'm sixteen," said Jocelyn.

"I'm fifteen. Well, almost sixteen. Nearer to sixteen

than fifteen," Meline added. She took one foot out from under her and sat on the other one.

"Really," said Jocelyn, "it is extraordinary how you always sit with one leg under you. Like some kind of stork. Are you *hatching* your feet?" Jocelyn placed her knife and fork together on a diagonal in the center of her plate and sat back, looking as if she were done with dinner and us as well. Meline and I looked at her in amazement. It was not like her to be so rude. Then Meline peered down at her foot as if expecting a baby bird to indeed come crawling out of it. She put both feet on the floor and seemed disturbed.

I spied Meline's plate with all its leftovers and nearly untouched brisket and said, "Aren't you hungry?"

"I had a lot of chocolate," she said.

"Ah," I replied happily. I was quite pleased that my solution had worked. When I had noticed the hot dog dinners were not being greeted with enthusiasm I tried to think what I could use to tempt the girls' apparently capricious appetites and remembered that a woman I had met at a conference had told me that women were crazy for chocolate. That they would do anything for the stuff. I remember standing back and looking at her searchingly, speculating on just how crazy she was. Then I promptly forgot the whole business, but with two hungry but appetiteless nieces this conversation had come back to me. What was the name of that chocolate this woman had spoken so lovingly of, oh yes, Godiva. I got on the Internet and ordered the girls each twelve boxes to be sent overnight. That should hold them. That should keep them from starving to death. I had Sam, the helicopter pilot, deliver them. He accepts all my mail and deliveries at his address in Vancouver and then drops them on the island when the mood seizes him. Sam likes being a delivery service, although he really isn't very good at it, mostly because he can only manage to drop my mail and deliveries in *roughly* the direction of the house. I never complain and, in fact, don't find my packages half the time, but then, I often don't remember ordering things, so I suppose it doesn't matter.

Anyhow, when the chocolates arrived, I could tell from the rattling sand sound in the boxes that, because of Sam, they were broken to bits. But girls weren't fussy about the shape their chocolates were in, were they? That woman at the conference made it sound as if, given a choice, they would just inject them directly into their veins anyway. I'd found one of the boxes in a rabbit hole. It was rather like an Easter egg hunt, I thought happily. I found some other things Sam had "delivered" randomly about the island as I went around hunting for the Godiva boxes, and they came as a pleasant surprise, as if they had sprung out of the earth spontaneously. The reverse of spontaneous combustion, I thought with amusement. Sometimes my own temperament and lifestyle suited me so exactly that I felt a wave of contentment wash over me. If only people would stop fussing. If they would enjoy the things that happened to them in the serendipitous way they occurred instead of worrying that they weren't happening the way they were *supposed* to happen, they'd surely be a lot more content with life. All those people I met at conferences who were always off to the gym in the hotel or doing something equally improving. Improve yourself to what end, I always wanted to know. What was it that people wanted to *be*?

"Well," I said, pleased that Meline had enjoyed her chocolates, "interesting dinner." Forgetting that the interesting part had all been happening in my head and they hadn't been privy to it. It occurred to me again that once you started making contact with people they wanted *you* to listen to *them* and the whole thing became exhausting. Positively exhausting.

"Who wants cake?" Mrs. Mendelbaum, her mouth full of kugel, called from the kitchen, where she was eating standing up at the kitchen table while making a grocery list.

"What?" I asked. "Did you say something, Mrs. Mendelbaum?"

There was a pause while she swallowed. "I said who wants cake? A nice little piece of honey cake, maybe?"

"Are you still eating in there?" I called back.

"I shouldn't eat?"

"No, no, that's not what I meant. I keep telling you, dear lady, you don't have to eat in there like some kind of fugitive. Why will you not join us here at table? I'm sure the girls wouldn't mind."

"Mind? What's to mind?" yelled Mrs. Mendelbaum. "Poor little things lose their parents, the only living things they have in the world, and they should care if I eat with them?"

"It would be good for them is what I meant to say. I'm no great shakes at keeping them company. A woman at the table would be . . . an *asset for us all.*" My voice trailed off at this last. Good manners demanded such a response that would further imprison me in intolerable company, but I choked it out in a desperate victory of principle over desire.

"A woman, why a woman? I should menstruate on them?" She was muttering to herself, unaware that we could hear her quite clearly, that poor little Jocelyn was turning red. "Now listen, Mr. Smarty Pants," said Mrs. Mendelbaum, raising her voice so we would hear her and slapping out the "t"s in "smarty pants" in her most acid German accent, putting all her derision into that consonant, "so I read. So I know. The cook does not eat with the family. Don't think I didn't see that book you planted in the kitchen—*What Does a Butler Do?* What does a cook do, one whole chapter. What does a footman do? Who heard of such things, Mr. Fancy Pants? A cook, the book says, does not eat at table. A cook eats in the kitchen."

"Could I *be* more welcoming?" I whispered anxiously. "It isn't I, is it, that is instigating this ridiculous argument? I could not be more democratic. Not that there is a need for it. Of course everyone should eat together. But she is going to be temperamental, after all. I hoped not— but I feared. I read about that in that very book of which she speaks. So many cooks *are* temperamental. It is, after all, called the culinary *arts*."

"You see, you should have interviewed, and not just picked the first one that came along. You might have discovered this ahead of time," whispered Jocelyn.

In a louder voice I called, "I swear to you, Mrs. Mendelbaum, I didn't plant a book about servants in the kitchen so that you would find out that cooks don't eat with the family. I didn't plant any books anywhere. Well, that is, I did put books about in logical places, but not with any idea that anyone but me would read them. I didn't plan to have anyone else living here. You all just . . . showed up."

"Showed up, just showed up, did I?" muttered Mrs. Mendelbaum and ate a second piece of kugel, ignoring us in the dining room and finishing her list. "Crazy man." She ate a few more bites and then shouted to the dining room, "My Mendel was a student! Educated!"

I didn't know what to make of this. We waited. It sounded like the beginning of an accusation, but nothing else was forthcoming. We sat and looked at each other around the table for a few minutes silently and then all said at the same time, *"Mendel Mendelbaum?"*

"*I'm sorry*, Mrs. Mendelbaum. You must believe me when I say I had no *idea* that book was going to give you such ideas. Please throw it on the fire immediately or get rid of it in any way that satisfies you. I don't remember half of what is in this house. All you have to do is clean it to find that out." I thought this was a very satisfactory and ameliorating thing to say, but it only seemed to ruffle Mrs. Mendelbaum all the more.

"So now you are suggesting I don't clean properly? I'll clean it all right!" shouted Mrs. Mendelbaum threateningly.

"She told me earlier she wasn't feeling well and her feet hurt," whispered Jocelyn to us from mid-table.

"Please come eat with us. I beg you to eat with us. I'm *dying* for you to eat with us," I said, now stuck in a landslide of cascading and escalating entreaties, each one more insincere than the last.

This is what comes from having people living with you. It all comes down to doing strange things, crazy things, such as entreating someone to do something which clearly neither one of you wants in an attempt to convince that person of the affection you do not feel for them and which, in any case, they don't want, in a further attempt to do no harm or ameliorate the harm you unknowingly did. We should all live alone on islands.

There was a long pause from the kitchen as if Mrs. Mendelbaum was thinking it over. Finally she said, "I don't like sitting down to such big heavy meals. Es brent mir ahfen hartz. I bloat."

Well, that certainly made me sorry I had brought it up. When I wasn't feeling vaguely sorry for Mrs. Mendelbaum, another victim of bad luck and circumstances, her whole family having predeceased her, she drove me crazy. Then I felt guilty for being driven crazy. What kind of heartless man is driven crazy by someone like poor, unfortunate Mrs. Mendelbaum? And why should I have to think of her at all? All I really needed to do was pay her salary. It was all so inconvenient. I had gotten her so I wouldn't have to think about food and could keep my mind on my research, but now I found myself thinking about Mrs. Mendelbaum. I would never get any work done this way. And all because my nieces had to eat. And what kind of thoughts were *these*? To be unable to sit down to dinner with my own nieces without resenting it? To resent having to think about feeding them? "I'm a *monster*. A *monster!*" I said aloud to myself, forgetting as usual what was in my head and what could be heard. Forgetting even anyone's presence at the table with me. I had already forgotten the girls, the dining room was so dark, ill lit, with its massive table, Meline a good twenty feet from me and pale, washed-out, little bony Jocelyn hardly noticeable in any setting, so thin and watery-looking. I pushed my chair out from the table and stumbled off to bed.

Mrs. Mendelbaum came in as I was leaving. "Cake, anyone?" she asked.

MELINE

SIX WEEKS AFTER LANDING on the island, when the fog of our suddenly changed circumstances had had a chance to clear out of our heads, I realized Jocelyn and I would have to find something to do. The helicopter kept dropping off books and school supplies from the distance education program that my social worker had enrolled us in when she was making our arrangements with Uncle Marten. It was what most of the island-raised children did, she reported. But, given Sam's hit-or-miss delivery system, sometimes we found the supplies and sometimes we didn't. Neither one of us felt competent to hit the books yet, so the books and workbooks tended to sit around the house, still wrapped in plastic, wherever we tossed them after finding them on the ground by the house. When Uncle Marten came across them, more often than not he heaved them on the fire that was always roaring in the huge fireplace in the living room. Keeping the fire stoked was supposed to be one of Mrs. Mendelbaum's jobs, but she was too delicate to spend the day heaving giant logs in, so we all, even Uncle Marten, took turns. Uncle Marten didn't recognize the books as our schoolbooks and only saw them as rather cheaply bound things and wondered why he had gotten them. "What's this garbage?" he would say, picking up a math workbook and chucking it into the flames. So even when we did periodically pick up a book and halfheartedly start a course of study, we'd find bits missing, textbooks or workbooks or worksheets, so that it was impossible to piece together where you were in the lesson and what you were supposed to do next, and eventually we just gave up. Giving up seemed like the logical conclusion for every endeavor in those days. Nothing seemed worthwhile. Everything ended eventually anyway.

The last time Jocelyn and I had seen each other was when I was nine. Her family had taken a vacation and visited us on Cape Cod. I remembered little about her from that except that she was lean and blond and quiet and not much fun. Heading out to the island to live with her, I had expected we would like each other much better than originally because we now had our shared tragedy as a common bond and would be in sympathy with each other in a way no one else could quite understand. But we were not. Jocelyn didn't seem to be in need of any sympathy and she certainly didn't want mine. Most of the time her face was hard and tight and her lips appeared set in cement. If I smiled at her she looked mortally offended as if I were trying to lure her, seduce her to join me in my slovenly ways. So now, after six weeks of stilted, uneasy conversation when it took all my self-control to keep from chucking things at her, we kept a polite distance.

I spent a lot of time pacing around the house, itching for something to do, anything to keep me occupied but nothing that required too much concentration. Meanwhile every day at two o'clock precisely, Jocelyn put on her winter coat, which like mine was wool and completely inappropriate, and went trudging out into the driving rain.

At first I paid no particular attention, but as the days dragged on I got curious. What did she do out there? Why always at two o'clock? Was she meeting someone? No, that was ridiculous. There was no one else on this island. It was just the four of us and a lot of rain. Still, it was odd, and I hadn't pegged Jocelyn as the type to do odd things, so one day I decided to follow her. I waited until she was across the meadow, then put on my heavy wool coat and slipped out behind her. By the time I had made it to the cover of the woods I was drenched and muddy. I had to race a bit after that to see where she was going, but even though I made a lot of noise she didn't seem to notice, so intent was she on her mysterious, intensely purposeful mission. She looked very melodramatic and *Wuthering Heights*. She *could* be a gothic heroine, I thought to myself, one who came to no good end. Then I decided she wasn't sympathetic enough to be the heroine. She'd make a better head of orphanage or strange housekeeper entrusted with the master's dark secret. She had the pinched expressions for it. When we got to the top of a hill, she sat down in the clearing, pulling her knees up to her chest. Then I could not have been more surprised by what came next: she put her head down on her knees and started to sob. Did she come here every day to this spot, getting soaked, just to sit in the mud and weep?

I thought about speaking to her. Telling her that sobbing on a hillside at two o'clock every day was about as bad a habit as a person could fall into, but even that seemed to take more energy than I had lately. And it only underscored for me the painfully obvious fact that if she had time for this, we simply didn't have enough to do. I turned to go, but *that*, in the annoyingly contradictory way she did everything, was when she finally noticed me.

"You! Are you following me?" she asked, tapping me on the shoulder from behind and causing me to cry out. "I didn't mean to startle you, but I don't want to be spied on."

"You know, Jocelyn, if we had more to do, you wouldn't have the luxury of sobbing on a hillside every day at exactly two o'clock. I was thinking we should find something to do because crying doesn't do any good."

"You ate all your chocolates in just a few days. I suppose you thought that was going to make it all go away?"

"I was hungry."

"Leave me alone."

Eating all the chocolates like that *was* an indulgence in grief. But it seemed pointless to bicker about these things. We didn't talk to each other at all after that. Sometimes, when politeness doesn't work, bluntness finds a way into the heart and a friendship is formed. But this time I could see nothing; not even a pile driver was going to break down the wall between us. We had no real relationships, any of us. We had no one on the island. We were each of us entirely alone.

MARTEN KNOCKERS

ALL THIS SILENCE suited me fine. My take on it was that the girls had finally settled down, and I ate my way quite happily through the silent dinners, the better to think about where Einstein had gone so irrevocably wrong. As no one seemed to want to talk, I felt justified in reading at the table again, a practice I had sorely missed. But Mrs. Mendelbaum apparently didn't *like* silence and came to me at teatime in my study. She was always coming to me with problems during tea because she brought my tray to me and clearly thought it was the perfect opportunity to ambush me in my lair. It almost made me abandon my afternoon tea, and I would have if I wasn't so badly in need of caffeine and sugar at that hour to keep my brain pumped until dinner.

"Sir," she began.

"I told you not to call me that," I said irritably. "My

name is Marten. Or if you must, Mr. Knockers. But *not*, I beg you, 'sir.' It makes my skin crawl."

"A little word—"

"You always want a little word with me about something," I groaned. "And it's always when I'm in the middle of some perplexing problem like trying to find the missing ingredient in the unified field theory."

"Oh, who can think of such things!"

"Well, I can, Mrs. Mendelbaum, I'd say that's rather obvious. But you'd have me switch from thinking about something important like trying to discover the force that ties together all the energy in the universe and instead think about something like we're out of sugar again and the milk hasn't arrived."

"It arrives. It arrives squashed. Milk everywhere in the ground but not in the carton. By you this is a small problem?"

"All right, whatever it is, get it over with. I don't want to argue about the milk endlessly. I contracted for a helicopter to make my deliveries, and if there are bugs in the system, well, there are bugs in any system. The house is the system I hired *you* to fix. The universe is the system *I'm* trying to fix. If everyone would just stick to their own system, I'm sure everything would turn out just fine. But I can see you are going to invite me in to solve another problem that I hired *you* to solve. So go ahead. What is it this time?" I asked, putting down my pen with a great deal of dramatic resignation, which seemed to be lost on her.

"There is something wrong with the girls. Such quiet!"

"Well, that's hardly any of our business, Mrs. Mendelbaum."

"Not our business? Whose business should it be, I'd like to know? The thin one, what's her name?" Mrs. Mendelbaum was always forgetting people's names. She seemed to know who people were, so I wondered if the North American names simply didn't register on her. Perhaps she would remember them if she could rename us familiar names from her youth. Did we all have a data bank of familiar, easily accessible information garnered in our youth and not added to after, say, our teens? I made a note on a piece of scrap paper about returning to this idea with a possible end to writing a paper on it. This seemed to infuriate Mrs. Mendelbaum, who barked, "Hert zich ein!"

"Jocelyn, I think," I said, absentmindedly, still scribbling away, not a clue in the world what she'd just barked.

"Is she sick, I wonder? She hardly eats, that one. A bird she's the size of."

"Well, girls *like* to be thin, don't they? They watch their figures. Do it on purpose, I believe. When they're not cramming chocolates down their gullets like Strasbourg geese, they starve themselves. It's not a nice way to live, I admit, but it's apparently what you have to look forward to if you've been born without a Y chromosome. I didn't create the system. You must have been a girl once, Mrs. Mendelbaum, surely you can remember. Besides, I don't know what else to do for them. I *gave* them chocolate," I said, putting my pen down.

"They don't like each other, those two," said Mrs. Mendelbaum, ignoring me.

"Well, we all have to make adjustments, my dear woman," I said, very nearly adding, After all I don't like *you*. But I caught myself in time.

"Go. Go and have a little talk with them."

"*Me?*" I yelped, horrified.

"Who else?"

"Well, you're the one who noticed it," I argued. "If it's even true. I prefer to think that things are just in a calm. Yes, a calm ebb. Everything ebbs and flows. Soon it will flow and there will be noise again. Right now we are experiencing a calm ebb." I hoped that this sudden new theory could be true. It would keep humans manageable for me. But Mrs. Mendelbaum would not let me have it.

"Are you CRAZY?" she screeched. "ZEY ARE AT VAR!" When Mrs. Mendelbaum became particularly agitated, her German accent grew thicker and stronger. It seemed to be tied to her emotions, and the stronger her emotions, the stronger it became.

70

"Well, then *zey*, I mean *they*, will have to work it out. If you don't agree, then *you* go talk to them," I said, quite reasonably.

"I'm just the cook," said Mrs. Mendelbaum with finality.

"Now, now, you mustn't think of yourself in those terms. I'm sure you're a person in your own right," I said, wondering when I had gotten the job of counseling distraught servants with inferiority complexes. The next thing you knew, I'd have a shingle on my door and a long line of disgruntled workers with low self-esteem. It did not pay to be too good at this sort of thing. "Go on, now. Go have a little word with them. I'm sure you're better at it than I am. You're a woman, after all."

"Again with the woman business! He has the nasty habit of giving women credit for being better at anything he does not want to do himself," muttered Mrs. Mendelbaum, turning her head to look at the wall behind her. *Who* was she talking to when she did this? "It should all fall on me, maybe? The cleaning, the cooking, now the child raising?" she asked me.

"Well, you can't expect me to do it. *You* brought it up." Honestly, I thought, it was as if we were married and these were *our* children we were arguing over. No wonder I'd remained a bachelor. Imagine having to deal with someone constantly like this because you'd committed yourself to a lifetime of conversation about such things.

Imagine getting into bed at night, knowing you were in for not putting your head on a cool pillow and drifting off, wrapped in the luxury of your own stream of consciousness, but a barrage of someone else's daily leftovers, all their hopes and dreams and desires and fears and angers and thoughts. All coming at you. And you were supposed to pay attention to *that*. And *that* was what people got married for, threw their fortunes in with each other, that and sex, I supposed, but it really really was not worth it. I didn't understand it at all. How did people *live* like that? "*I* didn't mind the quiet. God knows *I* wasn't complaining. Now, I have an awful lot to do here. I know it doesn't look it when you come in and find me just staring into space, biting on pens and such—"

"It looks meshugeh," said Mrs. Mendelbaum. "Do you know what that means?"

"Yes, Mrs. Mendelbaum, I know what that word means," I said curtly.

"Well, that's what it looks. Meshugeh, if you ask me."

"I am *thinking* when I'm doing that. At least, I was until you came along."

Mrs. Mendelbaum rolled her eyes again. "So you'll talk to the girls?"

"Oh, all *right*. But I have no idea what you want me to say."

"Just have a little word. Is that so bad?"

"Well, it really does seem so intrusive to me," I began.

"And another thing," said Mrs. Mendelbaum "And you

could listen for a minute, maybe? Not scribble away, leaving me here, holding this farkuckt teapot?"

"Yes, yes, yes," I said impatiently, dying to do just that.

"I can't keep running this house alone, doing everything myself. Am I six people? Eleven bedrooms the man has. Oy, the dust bunnies alone! And six bathrooms. All that grout! A living room you could drive a truck through! Three floors!"

"I know the size of my own house," I snapped. "Approximately."

"I need a butler."

"You need a butler?" I repeated in astonishment. "What for?"

"*You* need a butler," Mrs. Mendelbaum amended. "To answer the door. I should answer the door on top of everything else?"

"But no one ever comes. We live on an *island*," I pointed out. "If we hired someone to answer the door he'd have nothing to do. Really, Mrs. Mendelbaum, you must be completely dotty."

"He can pick up the dropped packages for one thing and solve for us the problem with milk. They can only drop the cartons out of helicopters at such a height? He can organize the girls and share in the worrying. I should be the only one to worry?"

"What worry?"

"I worry."

"So you want me to hire a butler. One more person when I was perfectly happy living alone. So that he can help you worry."

"I don't want him to help me worry more. I want him to do the worrying. So I can worry less."

"Really, Mrs. Mendelbaum, you should be married. You seem so resolutely determined to do things as a pair that are perfectly well done alone."

There was a silence as I recalled that Mrs. Mendelbaum *had* been married and *had* had a family, but they'd all died. Maybe it was tactless to bring it up. But good Maud, people *do* die, I thought uncomfortably. They die every day. She should have gotten used to it by now. Mrs. Mendelbaum said nothing, and for a moment it was as if she wasn't there anymore. All her energy seemed to have left her. I liked the deflated Mrs. Mendelbaum even less than the annoying one. "Anyhow, now *I'm* beginning to worry because all this is beginning to make sense. Please leave me before it does. But let me ask you something, Mrs. Mendelbaum, if you get this butler you're so anxious for, do you think you could talk to *him* more and *me* less?"

Mrs. Mendelbaum came back from whatever place she had gone to and nodded.

"And is a butler above a cook, status-wise?"

"Who knows such things?"

"I thought you'd been reading books about servant protocol, but never mind," I said hastily, remembering that the last time we'd discussed servant protocol Mrs.

Mendelbaum had gotten touchy and shouted at me. I did not want to start that again. "What I want to know is if I give the butler an order to keep you away from me, could he order you to do that?"

"I suppose," said Mrs. Mendelbaum uncertainly.

"And have you direct your comments and complaints to me through him so that I deal with him? Could *he*, for instance, bring me tea?"

Mrs. Mendelbaum furrowed her brow in consternation as if she was trying to decide whether or not she liked the implication here, but before she could speak I said, "Good. Then start advertising. Now please go away and don't bother me until dinner."

"You'll have a little word with the girls?"

"YES! YES! NOW GO!" I said, and Mrs. Mendelbaum left looking satisfied.

"It's all going to hell," I said to myself. "It's all going to hell in a hand wagon. Oh, but unified fields . . ." as new possibilities occurred to me and I became lost once more in thought, mercifully forgetting Mrs. Mendelbaum and butlers and nieces and everything else.

But no matter how lost in thought I might be, I knew I would have to behave honorably and keep my promise at dinner, so after several false starts when I put down the book I was reading, looked at the girls, and picked up the book again, I finally leaped in with "Jocelyn, please pass the peas." There, half accomplished, I said to myself happily. This was going very well. This was going very well indeed. It would soon be all over. Then, "Meline, enjoying the chicken? Excellent." Ah, done, thank goodness. Imagine, starting a conversation in the middle of a perfectly good silence. It was madness. What was my world coming to? Then I stumbled off to bed. The next day at tea Mrs. Mendelbaum came tearing in.

"I thought I'd gotten rid of you," I said.

"WHAT? Gotten rid of me? You should only get rid of me and see what you would be eating then, Mr. Smarty Pants."

"What do you want now? Have you advertised for a butler?"

"A little talk with the girls, he promises."

"I did talk to the girls. I said, 'Please pass the peas' and something else. If they didn't want to jump on the conversational bandwagon, well, you can hardly blame me for that, can you, my dear Mrs. Mendelbaum?" I did not think her dear at all but was hoping to soothe her with my professorial charms and so get rid of her. That was the ticket. Did I have any professorial charms, I wondered. Well, we would find out.

"By you two sentences is a conversation?"

"I will *not* become the Mussolini of the dinner table even to please you, Mrs. Mendelbaum. If the girls do not wish to talk, so be it. Silence is golden. A thought you might even wish to ponder, Mrs. Mendelbaum."

"A talk is a talk. 'Pass the peas' is not a talk. 'Do you like chicken' is not a talk. A tomb it is here. A tomb. I

76

did not leave a tomb to come to another tomb. So fix it or make your own miserable messes, mister."

This stopped me in my tracks. First because "miserable messes, mister" was more alliteration than I would have ever given Mrs. Mendelbaum credit for coming up with. And second because Mrs. Mendelbaum had never called me "mister" before and I could not for the life of me figure out what this presaged. She was constantly surprising me in small ways.

"Ahem." I cleared my throat because I could think of no response, but felt I had to retain the verbal upper hand. "I see. Well, I will try once again, but I don't know how I can guarantee you a certain noise level. It seems a most unreasonable request."

But Mrs. Mendelbaum seemed satisfied with my promise, so at dinner I fussed with my potatoes and pushed about my salad and cut my meat into tiny pieces and thought, What in the world am I going to say to these two little statuelike creatures? Finally I looked up and said, "Ahem. Have I told you about the island?"

Jocelyn and Meline put down their forks and looked at me expectantly.

"When I left Wall Street I knew I wanted to buy an island here off the coast of British Columbia. I investigated what was available, whole islands being in rather short supply, as you can imagine. Most of the ones for sale were too small and dull or so remote that to have any deliveries made and to get on and off them was too complicated. Finally my realtor found this one, which he didn't think I would be interested in. It had a bad reputation, covered with debris, tragic history, etc. But I found it much more topographically interesting than the others, as you can see, meadows and beaches and woods and hills. It had been a training camp for pilots a long time ago. What are now the meadows had been dirt runways. They were trying to teach pilots to land in difficult circumstances, and the island was ideal for that as they could also teach them to land on water. Then one day a new commander was put in charge and took the idea of teaching the pilots to land under adverse circumstances a bit too far. He decided the pilots should learn to fly and land without radar or any instruments at all but by the seat of their pants. He insisted it could be done. That pilots could be trained without all the fancy equipment they had come to rely on, all their *crutches*, as he put it. All the things you sissy boys seem to think you need, he said to them. He didn't tell the air force this, mind you. He didn't tell anyone what he was doing. He just calmly stripped all the small planes in his command of their instruments and began his own small corps of what he claimed would be the most powerful fighting force anyone in the air had ever seen because *his* pilots could fly anywhere under any circumstances. He called it the Corps of the Bare-Boned Plane.

"The first week out, three pilots died. Everyone was crashing, but no one was coming to the island to shut down the operation. Because he wasn't reporting the

78

deaths. And his corps didn't even suspect that he wasn't reporting the deaths. They just thought this was what they had been sent to do. No one could escape. They were on an *island*. They were *stuck*. It was crash your plane on the island or crash it trying to escape. It wasn't as if they could swim to shore. You know what the waters are like around here. You can't swim without a wet suit. And even then it's iffy. No, it was a hell of an unfortunate set of options for those boys. Eventually, of course, one of the pilots figured out that it wasn't the military who had set this whole thing up, that the Corps of the Bare-Boned Plane was simply a bug up the nose of this one man, his own pet project, and that even the air force wouldn't let this kind of training go on if they knew about it—eleven pilots had died, and seven planes had been wrecked beyond repair. So when a new shipment of recruits arrived via helicopter this pilot stowed away and headed back to tell his superiors what was going on."

I stopped talking and went back to cutting up my meat in little pieces and thinking about binary equations. Had I told them enough? Nobody ever told anyone everything. Why should they? Why did meat have to come in such inconvenient chunks?

"But what happened to the mad commander?" asked Jocelyn.

"Oh, they put him away. Somewhere he couldn't do any harm. Away from his men. Away from his family. They pulled all the troops off the island and sent them elsewhere and this island just sat abandoned and forgotten, an embarrassment, a testimonial to what can go wrong. And then while I was island-shopping, the Department of National Defence put this island up for sale along with its other surplus, and I bought their island of wrecked planes and wrecked men."

"They sound more than wrecked, they sound smooshed," Meline said, eating her meat. "They sound blood-and-gutsed. They sound like a bunch of moldering corpses. They did *bury* them, didn't they, in their haste to clear out?"

"Oh . . ." groaned Jocelyn, putting down her fork. "Can we change the subject?"

"I would assume so, Meline," I said, not listening anymore and picking up a math journal to continue reading an article. I'd never found math interesting before, but it was! It was terribly interesting. At any rate, I figured I'd more than fulfilled my promise to Mrs. Mendelbaum, and you could only expect a man to do so much. Enough was enough. Now for some sensible thoughts. Then, forgetting I was in the middle of dinner, so engrossed was I in the article I was perusing, I got up, still reading, and trotted back toward my room.

"Got in himmel!" said Mrs. Mendelbaum. She was still muttering to herself from the doorway as I was leaving. "Such talk! You ask for a talk and you get such talk! Such talk to give a soul nightmares maybe. By him this is a healing talk? A conversation starter maybe? Oy. I'll bring them some cake. A taste. Who wouldn't feel better with a bit of cake?" She went back to the kitchen, to cut cake, I suppose. Well, there are those who think the answer lies in undiscovered knowledge and those who think it lies in cake.

MELINE

"JOCELYN," I said the next day at two o'clock. I had followed her across the meadow to join her as she sobbed on her hillside. "I've been thinking we need something to do, and it might interest you to know that I know how to build a plane."

She stopped weeping for a second and glared at me. "You do not."

"Yes, I do. And I know how to fly a plane and I know you do, too. Now, what kind of possibilities does that bring to mind?"

"Oh, you do not know how to build a plane. Maybe you've seen the mechanics in your father's company *working* on a plane—"

"I can. I can build a vacuum cleaner, too. So could my mother. My father believed that if you used a tool you should understand it, and the best way to understand it was to know how to build it. We could build a plane. I could show you how. Now, according to Uncle, there are plane parts scattered all over the island. And we've got a lot of time and nothing to do."

"How are we going to move the parts even if we find them?" Jocelyn asked. "How are we going to get a bunch of scattered plane parts to one place?"

"I don't know. The first thing is to find them." I watched the wheels turn in Jocelyn's head, and for a second I saw a glimmer.

But even so she wasn't immediately available for the project. She had to rethink it constantly. She spent lots of time turning it over in her mind. We would be sitting by the fire and she would be staring intently at the flames and suddenly say, "Well, where are we going to build it without it being seen?"

"The barn back behind the house is empty."

"How are we going to get the parts through the doorway?"

"Well, gosh, Jocelyn, it's a *barn* door."

"I don't think it can be done."

And I'd have to go over it all again slowly with certainty and confidence because she was always half a step away from backing out.

"It can be done. We find the plane parts, we take them into the barn, and we put them together."

"Again, why would your father teach you to build a plane?"

"To be ready for anything. Suppose I flew a plane alone

and crashed somewhere? I should be ready to fix it. I should know how to survive."

"My father didn't teach me that when he taught me to fly," said Jocelyn. I shrugged. Her forehead was screwed up. "My father didn't seem to think he needed to prepare me for such things." I shrugged again. Then her tone stopped being ruminative and became shrill. "And he was right! Because nothing like that happened to me. And what happened to you and what happened to me couldn't be prepared for, so it's a waste of time trying to prepare anyone for anything. Anyhow, we build the plane and then what?"

My mind went to the moment of liftoff. That second when miraculously you leave the earth behind. When you're up above it all. Removed. Out of reach.

"And also," she said, her shoulders slumping, folding in on herself again, "do you have any idea how much plane parts weigh? Even very small planes?"

"We'll need some kind of dolly. We'll need all kinds of things, Jocelyn. Soldering irons probably. Or, who knows, maybe we'll get lucky and find a plane that's not in such bad shape and just needs some repairs. I mean, until we start looking, we don't know what we'll find."

"Even if we make a plane, we might not be able to fly it."

My mother had taught me that if you could think it, you could do it. That's why my mother had such hopes for the guesthouse in Zimbabwe. It never occurred to her that she couldn't make it happen. She wanted it so badly that that in itself became a kind of faith. My mother's faith had been so strong that her beliefs created my universe, too. I realized that what we may think is incontrovertible knowledge of what is, is only made up out of our beliefs. When she died with all those things she was so sure she would do undone, all these beliefs collapsed for me. The universe was not what my mother believed it to be. I could not hang my hat there anymore. I didn't know what to believe in now. Somehow, as much as I had been sure about my mother, my mother who was so loving, who surely must be in touch with what was, so clearsighted, so good was she, despite all that, she had gotten it all wrong. She hadn't known any more than anyone else. Because I found it hard to believe that this was possible, I harbored a half hope that it had been a mistake, they hadn't died, it must be that my mother and father had somehow survived without anyone knowing, that they weren't buried in foreign soil but were perhaps making their way through the Zimbabwe countryside to me and anytime now I would see them again.

"Jocelyn, suppose our parents aren't dead?" I asked suddenly and, as soon as I said it, was sorry.

"They're dead," said Jocelyn flatly and got up and left the fire.

Mrs. Mendelbaum began interviewing butlers shortly after that. Although when Sam delivered *us*, he put me and Jocelyn and Mrs. Mendelbaum on the ground, a sop to our femininity perhaps, he treated the butlers as milk and dropped them wherever he felt like it from a hanging insubstantial-looking ladder. Jocelyn and I would be scouring the fields for airplane parts and hear the whirring blades of a chopper, and down a butler would come, bowler hat and all. At first the hats startled me and Jocelyn, and then we read Mrs. Mendelbaum's ad: *Butler wanted for large household of Mr. Marten Knockers. Must have experience. And proper clothes. Including the butler hat.*

I was amazed at the number of men who showed up to be interviewed. I don't believe I would go to an interview for a job in which they asked you to bring "the butler hat." I told Mrs. Mendelbaum that she had a better chance of getting a higher-class butler if she called it a bowler. "You know, Mrs. Mendelbaum, so many of these bowler hats look brand-new. I think they buy them just for the interview. I think what you've got here is not a lot of experienced butlers but a lot of out-of-work waiters with new hats."

"But you zee! Zey come. Zey all want the work," she said, pointing out the window at a newly arriving candidate who was hanging from the helicopter ladder, calling imprecations up to Sam. His fist was raised and his face was red, and really you couldn't blame him, it wasn't one of Sam's better hoverings. The ladder skimmed the ground around and around in a ten-foot radius.

"I hope he doesn't fall," I said to Mrs. Mendelbaum.

We were sipping tea and she was getting out her list of interview questions from the kitchen table drawer.

"Never mind them, they are all alike," said Mrs. Mendelbaum.

"Haven't you found one you like?" I asked.

"Zey are little pansy boys dressed in their daddy's clothes. I need a man who can VORRY."

I didn't know what "vorry" was, and the butler was quickly approaching the door, so I left. It never did much good to talk to Mrs. Mendelbaum: half the time it was as if she wasn't listening and the other half she didn't seem to know what I meant. But she always offered us cake and tea.

I winced when I saw Mrs. Mendelbaum's list of questions. Jocelyn and I overheard several of Mrs. Mendelbaum's interviews when we were sitting by the fire. Interviewing made Mrs. Mendelbaum very nervous and caused her not only to lapse into her German accent but to speak a strange mix of German and English. "Site vem haf you butlering began?" and "Vee feel housen haf you been butler at?" If you spoke a bit of German, you might be able to figure out what she was asking, but so far none of them had. Some courageous souls, after trying to get her to paraphrase her questions, gave up altogether and simply made a stab at any kind of answer at all.

"Zey are all idiots," Mrs. Mendelbaum would moan after they left.

It didn't help that many of them were still shaking

from the helicopter ride and circus-ladder-type descent. One fellow, obviously thinking his arrival might be witnessed, as indeed it was, made a daring leap off the ladder, but he misjudged the distance and landed on his face in a large mud puddle from which there was no reclaiming his savoir faire. Mrs. Mendelbaum said nothing and gave him a dry pair of Uncle's pants and, after an extremely perfunctory interview in which none of us had a clue what she was asking, sent him back to the hill to wait for Sam. We saw him shivering there in the rain for an hour, holding up his too short, too wide pants. "She might at least have given him tea," sniffed Jocelyn.

"It's like she's looking for something specific in them and when she doesn't find it, she gets *angry*," I said, but I did not want to think about who people really were. All I wanted to do was keep busy and not think at all.

The butler interviews continued for two weeks. Some candidates handled them better than others. One threw up. Many of them lost their bowler hats in the descent from the helicopter and, when they weren't hired, wrote to Uncle Marten demanding he replace them or reimburse them.

Uncle Marten, who wasn't paying attention, as usual, came into dinner one night and said, "What are all these letters demanding hats? Money for hats? From perfect strangers. Is this some new kind of charity or someone's idea of a get-rich-quick scheme? Bilk the poor unsuspecting rich fellow for hat money? Is it a prank? Well, I won't have it. It's very annoying." And he threw them all in the fire. It would take a lot to get hats out of ole Marten Knockers, he told us, and right there made a vow he would *never* send anyone money for hats, no matter how plausible-sounding their claims. He rewarded himself with an extra piece of cake at dinner. "Girls," he said, "I am having extra cake because some days one is especially pleased with oneself. Some days one simply congratulates the universe for having one in it." Then he dug greedily into the cake, chocolate this time, and was so excited that he missed his mouth with his fork and actually stabbed himself in the chin. He had tine marks for a week.

One of the last interviews that Jocelyn and I overheard began with Mrs. Mendelbaum challenging the poor fellow, "ZO! You ZINK you vant to VORK on an *IS-LAND???*"

The butler, who was somewhat less intimidated than the dozen who had gone before, perhaps because he was British and had maybe even *been* a butler at some point, turned to us, who were sitting not far away by the fire, and said, "Good Lord, do you have any idea what she is trying to say?"

"Don't talk to ZEM. Zey are just silly gells," said Mrs. Mendelbaum.

"Seagulls?" said the poor man. "See here now, they are not seagulls. Dropped from a helicopter, told very ordinary young ladies are seagulls. I demand to speak to Mr. Knockers. It was Mr. Knockers's name on the advertisement."

"You vill zee NO ONE. NO ONE. I am in charge!" roared Mrs. Mendelbaum, getting up and putting her hands on her hips and for emphasis throwing on the floor the wet dishrag she'd been wiping down the kitchen with when he arrived. This seemed to stymie the man, who was swiftly losing his composure. He was at the mercy of a mad German woman on an island with no apparent way off. I could see his point completely. If she would only relax and offer them tea and cake instead of getting so nervous and shouting at them.

"Now listen, I'll just go, then," he said, getting up.

"Mit out your tea?" asked Mrs. Mendelbaum sweetly, sitting down again. She knew there weren't many applicants left, and whereas usually she would have been happy to see the back of this one—she never liked ones who quaked in the face of her fierceness, or gave up—she knew she had to choose someone soon or be out of luck, and who knew who would follow this one, so she was willing to make allowances.

"You're raving mad," said the butler and turned to me and Jocelyn again, asking us where the helicopter pickup was. We pointed to the hill, although we warned him that Sam wouldn't be back for another three hours. He looked at Mrs. Mendelbaum and looked at the rainy hill and chose the hill. I thought this showed good judgment, and she should have hired him on the spot. Jocelyn, when we were discussing this later, said that it showed a complete lack of character and anyone who couldn't deal with

Mrs. Mendelbaum would be completely undone by Uncle Marten.

"But Uncle Marten is kind," I argued. "I don't think Mrs. Mendelbaum is exactly."

"I don't think it's that she isn't kind," said Jocelyn.

"She throws the butlers out into the rain," I said evenly.

"She doesn't."

"Well, they always end up choosing the rain over her before she has the chance, but you know very well that *given* the chance she would throw them out into the rain."

"I don't think it's that she isn't kind," said Jocelyn, staring absently into the fire. "I think it's that she is afraid."

But when the quaking butler got back to the mainland he turned out to be one quaking butler who was not ready to let bygones be bygones. He e-mailed Uncle Marten and told him he planned to sue. He had been traumatized. He had been almost kidnapped as far as he was concerned and made to wait on a rainy hill, fearful for his life. Even Uncle Marten knew this was overstating things, but it still caused him to go downstairs to the kitchen and speak to Mrs. Mendelbaum. "You mustn't *scare* them, Mrs. Mendelbaum," he admonished. "It isn't nice."

"I? Scare them?" asked Mrs. Mendelbaum, snorting with derision. "A frail little Jewish lady? Pansy froufrou boys. They should know from scary."

"Nevertheless," said Uncle Marten, coughing gently.

But that was all he could think of to say, and he returned to his room defeated. Later at dinner Mrs. Mendelbaum, who felt unjustly accused, tried to bring it up again as she carried in the soup. "I shouldn't ask interview questions? I should maybe let them interview *me*?"

Uncle Marten gazed into his soup bowl with exaggerated interest. "There, there, what kind of soup did you say this was?"

But Mrs. Mendelbaum was not ready to let it go and insisted on carrying all the courses into the dining room while keeping going a running monologue about her own frailness and the unfairness of such accusations, the better to torment Uncle Marten, until he finally gave up, saying "I can't listen to any more of this. Do what you must. I've got particles on my mind. Articles about particles." And left the table.

"There you see!" said Mrs. Mendelbaum, turning triumphantly to us. "He is no GOOT to us anymore. He is RHYMING!" And she took away the dishes with a queer little smug smile on her face. Uncle Marten spent a lot more time in his room after that, and it was our impression he was avoiding seeing her ever again.

During all of this, we had been scouring the island and I couldn't believe that we hadn't found so much as a fuselage. "He must have made it up," I said for the umpteenth time to Jocelyn.

"He couldn't. He hasn't the imagination," she said.

"If he didn't make it up it's not because he hasn't the imagination. He has plenty of imagination. I think if he didn't make it up it's because he has too much respect for the truth."

"Uncle Marten must have seen the plane parts himself, then. Otherwise how would he know they were here? It's a big island and we haven't seen it all."

"He might not have seen them. He was told a bunch of pilots crashed small planes. He might have just assumed there were plane parts still around," I said, collapsing on a hillside and getting soaked again. We were always getting soaked. I felt like a fish. I thought we'd have a nice whiny time of it in the mud deploring the size of the island, but Jocelyn looked at me sitting in wet leaves, turned abruptly, and walked back to the house. I could never get used to how she didn't announce her intentions ever; when she wanted to go somewhere she just left without a word as if emphasizing the lack of connection between you. Her lack of obligation to you in the form of explanation, greetings, or closings or the usual grease of human interaction. I groaned and stood up on sore cold limbs and hobbled back behind her.

That night I awoke around 2 a.m. with an idea. I dressed quickly and, taking the flashlight that was beside my bed, went to Jocelyn's room and woke her. She screamed as soon as I touched her shoulder. I moved my hand swiftly over her mouth to muffle it, saying, "For heaven's sake get a grip," and she bit me.

JOCELYN

ALL WAS DARKNESS AND DREAMS when I suddenly awoke on a train to bright, uneven, moving light. Fire-light where there should be no fire and strange faces and screaming. Where were my parents? What were they do-ing to those women? Where was my mother?

"You'll have Mrs. Mendelbaum in here in a second if you don't shut up," hissed a voice as a hand clamped over my mouth.

I sat up in bed panting beneath it and then, having ap-parently bitten Meline's hand, gently pulled it away. A cold sweat dripped down under my arms beneath my loose nightgown and my eyes slowly adjusted to the fa-miliar furniture of the bedroom. Meline didn't seem to notice the state I was in, but I was used to this. No one else here had seen the fires or the bodies or the cast-off limbs. There were others there when it happened who were whisked off as quickly as I was, but even when I re-turned to identify bodies, I spoke to no one else who had been there that night. And then I was carried away as quickly as possible to safety as if geography could put dis-tance between me and what happened. As if I didn't live there now, every day. Your mind could be a country, I found out, and those around you made foreigners by an unshared memory.

"I had an idea," Meline was saying excitedly, looking bright-eyed and bushy-tailed as usual. She was always so energetic. As if she had no feelings to weigh her down. As if she didn't care what had happened. "We may have missed the airplane parts because over the years they've been covered with leaves which have composted. They may be the hills we've walked on. They may be camouflaged under bushes and brush. If there's bits of metal poking out though, light has a better chance of finding it than our naked eyes. We need dark and a flashlight to spot metal peeking out from beneath all that brush."

"It's the middle of the night. The whole idea was crazy to begin with anyway."

"So far," Meline pointed out, "all you've done since getting here is sit around and raise your eyebrows at people."

This took me aback. I had been mentally raising my eyebrows at people, it was true, but I had no idea it had been detected. This horrified me. I thought I had appeared scrupulously polite and kind. Sort of like Grace Kelly. "We'll probably get pneumonia, going out in the rain at night," I said quickly, leaping up and putting on my clothes to change the subject.

"Probably," said Meline cheerfully, handing me a flashlight.

MRS. MENDELBAUM

SUCH PEOPLE who come looking for work. The last says to me, "I'd rather dig ditches than work for the likes of you." Is this something you should say to a person? A feier zol im trefen. So that was that. No more applicants. No butler. Then, a brocheh, out of nowhere comes one more. But such a man. Like a corpse. So tall and thin. Does he eat, I ask myself? And such color. He has never seen the sun? Eyes so far back, looking out from the back of caves. Like he stands perhaps at the edge of the ocean and looks out over water at you. Oy, this one gives me the shivers. And no résumé! Who comes for a job with no résumé? All right, I had no résumé, but what did I know? And no hat, but this I overlook because at least he keeps his head like a man. The helicopter? Not a word. This one does not turn a hair. "Implacable," says Meline as we watch from the window. He climbs down the ladder. "Maybe that should have been in the ad." "Hush," I say to the girls. He should think this is a comedy club?

"Zo, your name is Humdinger?" I say when he arrives and tells us his name. "Sit. How long have you a butler vanted to be, Mr. Humdinger?"

"How long have I, have I what, Mrs. Mendelbaum?"

All of them bad ears. Repeating, repeating, I spend all day repeating to them. So I repeat again.

"Well, never," says Humdinger.

So this answer is new. All of them before tell me they wanted at birth butlers to be. So, where do I go from here, I think? Should I ask him what he means by such an answer? Should I go on with questions? "Zo the next question, then. I zee you arrive mit out the hat?"

"I don't believe I own a hat, Mrs. Mendelbaum," says Humdinger.

"No hat? No hat?" Now I am confused. What should I say to such a person?

"I find a collar much more satisfactory," says this Humdinger, smiling even. "How are you, Mrs. Mendelbaum? How is it working out for you in this gentleman's employ?"

"How is . . . how is it for *me*, ahzes ponim?"

I look at this man. Yes, he looks very neat. A nice black suit, a little old maybe, a little threadbare, but this I don't mind, he has worked, this man, and almost a collar like the kind they call mandarin. What is with such a collar and no tie? Maybe I think he is more up to date with butler fashion. Maybe they wear collars and no hats now. This is practical. Hats can fall in soup when you make it. A hat on such a tall man can be knocked off in doorways. And it is a good question, how do I enjoy working for Mr. Knockers? He should only know. But still, how else can he find out what kind of man will maybe employ him? He is thinking of himself, this one, smart fellow.

"Of course, you are thinking of it from your end. But

still, no résumé, no appointment, what am I to think?" I ask him.

"Well, no résumé, no, but I did call Mr. Knockers to say I'd be stopping in for a brief visit, but he just said, Another one, and hung up. Is he about?"

"Feh, him!" I say. "Bal toyreh! He is not in charge. I am in charge. He tells me you are coming. A Humdinger. He cannot make out why. He does not say it is a person who wants the butler job. But does he remember from one day to the next? Well, perhaps you will see."

"I think maybe there has been a misunderstanding about my arrival," says Humdinger.

"Yes, yes, but we will overlook it. You should have sent a résumé. But you have not. And you have not the hat, but at least you have the collar. And you do not seem so afraid of me as these pansy boys who came before."

"No, but you see, Mrs. Mendelbaum," he begins again, but I will not let him. No, this one will not himself do in with silly prattle. So I stop him. He is the last chance. And he is not so bad, after all. He does not seem too much one for the fancy things. The types who come before, movies, books, the fashion plates they make of themselves. Don't think I don't know the type. This one looks as if he could worry.

"SO!" I make the sudden decision. My hands they slam down on the table to show this is final and I get up. "You are hired. No, not another wort! Ich hob es in drerd! I am exhausted. Ganz farmutshet. I am taking a nap."

MELINE

MRS. MENDELBAUM left a bemused Humdinger watching her disappear upstairs. Then he did a strange thing. He was putting his teacup by the sink, which was always stopped up, and he rolled up his sleeves, took the whole thing apart, fixed it, and then went upstairs to introduce himself to Uncle as the new butler.

"At least," said Mrs. Mendelbaum to us later with the least scorn she had expressed about any of them, "he wasn't a QUITTER." But we suspected she was willing to be more forgiving with him than the others because he was the last applicant.

"Best for last perhaps," said Jocelyn.

"Best or worst, him I was hiring. Your uncle never talks to me and not even a phone to use whenever I like. Just his radio phone, which I have to go up to that LAIR to ask for. No television. And how long can I listen to the radio?"

Mrs. Mendelbaum had tried for a week to convince Uncle Marten to buy a television set, but this he stood firmly against. "I won't have it. They're evil. Nothing kills off brain cells faster. They're noisy and they bring the entire world into your home. I've a good mind to throw that radio into the sea as well, and I will if I hear one more word about it." After that, Mrs. Mendelbaum was afraid to even talk to him for several days, and Jocelyn and I speculated that she hired Humdinger out of pure spite because every time Uncle Marten ran into him in the hallway, he jumped with fright. Humdinger did look like something that someone had dug up.

Humdinger didn't walk so much as he padded around like the cat he brought with him. He appeared suddenly behind you when you least expected. When he smiled, it was always at his own no doubt strange thoughts, barely a movement in his lips as if he had the neat trick of containing the smile within his eyes. As if even his *smile* was silent.

Because Humdinger insisted on slithering about so, we tended to forget about him, which seemed to suit him fine. When he spoke at all, it was to correct the pronunciation of his name, which none of us seemed to be able to get right either once we saw it spelled. He would correct and we would forget and he would correct again. It was Humdinger, "din" as in "dinner," "ger" as in "German." But the tendency was to want to call him Humdinger as in wasn't he just a real one. Eventually, though, we caught on, all except Uncle Marten, who never called him anything but Humdinger to rhyme with "ringer." Humdinger, after the first time, seemed to give up on him and never corrected Uncle. Jocelyn felt this was very bad for Uncle. She said she could see that he had been coddled and indulged, and that he didn't adhere to the manners the rest of us were supposed to. I guessed by that she meant me and her and Mrs. Mendelbaum, but she might as easily have meant the rest of the world. Jocelyn seemed to live by some pretty absolute standards.

Uncle Marten, once Humdinger arrived and succeeded in keeping Mrs. Mendelbaum busy and out of his hair, forgot all of us. He seemed to find it harder and harder to accept that the people who were on the island with him were not a temporary condition like houseguests or fleas but were going to be here for good. There would be no reprieve. So he locked himself more and more in his room, coming down only for meals and often working right through them, so that he wasn't really present for those either. It didn't matter to me and Jocelyn; we were up nights looking for airplane parts and, even though we slept late in the morning, were always tired. Our clothes never seemed to quite dry out, and I was afraid to use the dryer because it would attract Mrs. Mendelbaum's attention to how often we went out and how wet we got. So far no one seemed to have noticed we were going out at night.

MARTEN KNOCKERS

ONCE THIS FELLOW HUMDINGER ARRIVED, things seemed more orderly in the house, and Mrs. Mendelbaum began leaving me alone for more periods of time. Although I didn't like having people around, I oddly enough did begin to develop a certain fledgling affection for Humdinger's cat, who had been delivered by helicopter after Humdinger was hired. The cat, for some catlike reason of her own, decided that my hermitic temperament made me a soul mate and took to hanging out in my room with me, lying at my feet as I worked, or curling up on my desk or my bookcase. Once she tried to curl up on top of my head, perhaps because my bald head was so shiny and attractive. I always did think that a bald head, from a certain perspective, must be enticing. And now I had found out whose perspective it was. It was a cat's! Perhaps she thought she could be my missing hair. But, of course, it didn't work and the cat slid down my back, clawing for her life all the way, leaving huge scratch marks in my shirt, which made Mrs. Mendelbaum make caustic comments about my private life when she did the the laundry. She'd seen plenty when she was a girl in Vienna. Nothing would surprise her, she grumbled. Really, sometimes I did wonder about her past, but everyone has secrets and I had no desire to find out Mrs. Mendelbaum's. That *I* could hardly have much of a private life, living as I did, was of no matter to her. She knew mankind and its slippery practices. I seldom tried to change Mrs. Mendelbaum's mind about anything once she had taken a notion, which for her was apparently a process akin to pouring cement.

After the cat had scratched my back, whenever she came anywhere near my head, I would say, "Get away from me, you evil feline scratchy thing." Then I would open a tin of pull-top tuna I kept just for the kitty in my room. Imagine, I thought! Now I'm preparing meals for a cat! I supposed I would be making her her own goose for Christmas. Christmas!

I suddenly realized that Christmas would be in several weeks and I began to plan for it. Despite the fact that to most people the celebration of Christmas, if it involves anything, involves other people, and I, I must admit, don't *like* other people, I have a deep and abiding affection for Christmas. Every little Dickensian thing about it is splendid. I'm partial to plum puddings and deep Victorian purples and gold angels and Christmas tablecloths with red-and-green plaids and those candelabra where the reindeer antlers hold a dozen votive candles. Give me port and roasting chestnuts and spiced cider and gaily wrapped packages and stockings hung by the chimney with care and girls in velvet dresses and shiny patent leather Mary Janes and Handel's *Messiah* and Christmas carols and church music booming majestically through cathedrals. And bad weather and snuggling by the fire and unwrapping new books and eating too much candy and homemade cookies and old bad movies that I remember vaguely from my youth, since I'd never owned a television myself. I was very fond of all of it. Unfortunately, I never had any of this because you just don't do it when you live alone.

However, keeping one jaundiced eye on the cat that

rainy windy November afternoon when the fire was crackling and I watched out the window as Jocelyn and Meline tripped about the island peering into trees and bushes, which seemed to be their daily demented pursuit—you wouldn't catch me out on such a blustery day—it occurred to me that I now had a houseful of people, all of whom, presumably, would be wanting Christmas. Later it was pointed out to me that Mrs. Mendelbaum was Jewish and might prefer Hanukkah. It was the type of detail that often escaped me.

I was unusually happy and excited at the thought that I could finally have a nice old-fashioned Victorian Christmas. I would be indulging not just myself but the entire household. Perhaps my nieces wouldn't want green and red velvet bows attached to their heads, but there was always the cat . . . Yes, the cat. Perhaps we should get more cats. A . . . a *flock* of cats. All with velvet bows.

Christmas was the first upside to having a household that I had come across. And, of course, it is so nice to find an upside to *anything*, I always think. So every time I got stuck on the paper I was writing, and I seemed to get stuck quite a lot, perhaps because my mind would keep drifting back to Christmas, I would go on the Internet, which later would prove to be a thing of the Devil, so tempting was it, and order things. "I'll keep old Sam busy," I said to myself, ordering six velvet stockings, one for the cat (well, she was really an exceptionally *nice* cat), tree decorations, and a box of petits fours. As I really got in gear, the helicopter started dropping packages all over the place constantly, but unfortunately the wind carried many away or they got stuck in trees and rocky crevices and sometimes floated out to sea and were never seen again, and I would think months later, I wonder what happened to that box of popcorn balls I ordered, and where are the snowmen candles?

Meline and Jocelyn found quite a few boxes on their walks and would give them to Humdinger, who delivered them to me, and I would be forced to complain to Humdinger about the stupidity of companies sending me boxes of broken tree ornaments.

"You can't get good help anymore," agreed Humdinger.

It was becoming perfectly clear that Humdinger was the only person in the house besides myself with any sense. In fact, I really felt quite lucky to have found Humdinger. When I could remember who he was. Unfortunately, I did seem to run up against him in dark hallways quite a bit, and you really couldn't blame me for shrieking. The man does look like he walked straight out of one of those horror movies. What was the name of them, they were all alike, and they all seemed to have Boris Karloff in them somewhere. At any rate, it clearly never bothered him, although the girls seemed to think I might control myself, and you don't want to hear what Mrs. Mendelbaum had to say on the matter; after all, for years I had run into no one in my halls, so I could hardly be blamed for reacting when I seemed suddenly to be transported into *The Night of the Living Dead.* "Anyhow, go on now, keep Mrs. Mendelbaum out of trouble," I urged him.

"Very good," said Humdinger and padded back downstairs in his size-twelve Frankenstein shoes, which he nonetheless managed to make soundless.

Who is that man? I thought, already back to work on negative density. Oh, and I must remember to order a dozen crystal punch cups. There was, after all, a great deal to be done in the universe, and matter to be rearranged by ordering it from one place to another via the Internet. Our lives are full, only we never think about it, busy displacing matter from one place to the next, constantly rearranging the order of the cosmos with computers and mailboxes and money and little blips, making contact with people who fill these orders without ever knowing it, changing the shape of their days, changing the shape of warehouses, we are constantly affecting everything around us in the most mundane ways. We are all part of everything that moves, and most of it is so trivial. We think a sand dollar's life is trivial or a fly's, but look at our own. Why, it's all completely ridiculous. Oooo, I wonder if I remembered to order the marzipan fruits? They say there's a limited supply. Order soon. Why don't they just make more? People are extraordinary.

MELINE

As THE SOGGY DAYS went on and no airplane parts were found, I could see that Jocelyn was getting discouraged. She traipsed back into the house at 5 a.m. one morning, covered in twigs, and said, "Honestly, Meline, if we don't find an airplane part soon I'm going to stop this. It's too cold and I get too tired."

"What else are you going to do with your time?" I asked. "What are you saving your energy *for*? We'll just have to look *harder*!"

We didn't speak all day after that. She tired me with her languid negativity. She drooped about. I felt I constantly had to prod her to keep her on track. It didn't take a rocket scientist to see that the important thing was to BUILD THE AIRPLANE. And I was certain there were airplane parts out there. After dinner that night, which was silent because Uncle Marten was working on negative density, Humdinger never spoke unless spoken to, and Mrs. Mendelbaum had gone to bed early with a cold, Jocelyn and I had our dessert in the wing chairs by the fire.

Uncle Marten had suggested it as a way of getting rid of us in the oblique way he suggested things, saying, "Dessert together in the wing chairs before the fire. Now, that's what I'd do if I had a cousin and nothing better to do with my time," and had taken his up to his room, and now we sat there three feet apart but not speaking. I could have put my feet up on her chair, it was that close. I longed to do it if just to exasperate her. How could she sit so close to me and yet pretend so convincingly I wasn't even there? I wasn't looking for any kind of profound connection, but I didn't want her to act like I didn't exist. That was just weird. She ate her rice pudding methodically, and by the expression on her face she could have been sitting in a bus terminal, creating boundaries and fences around herself with the set of her body. You had the sense that if you tried to move in within three feet you would be zapped by invisible force fields.

"Have you noticed there seems to be a lot of new *stuff* around lately?" I asked suddenly, as my eyes moved away from her to the wing chair. "These chairs, for instance."

"These chairs were always here," she said calmly, wiping her mouth with the napkin she had brought from the table and placed upon her lap.

"Chairs were always here. These are new. The old ones were black or blue or something. These are cranberry and green and they match all those new candles on the mantel. And look, the bottom of the chairs still have leaves and twigs on them. These chairs have been *dropped* by helicopter."

"So Uncle Marten got some new chairs. So what?" asked Jocelyn.

"It's part of it all. There's new Christmas crap everywhere."

"I really wish you wouldn't use that word. My father really disliked it."

"My father used it all the time. You know, I'm finding it harder and harder to believe that our fathers were brothers."

"Or that Uncle Marten was brother to either of them," said Jocelyn.

This was true and opened up a whole new line of speculation for me. "Why do you suppose our fathers became pilots and Uncle Marten didn't?" I asked her. "And don't you think it's *strange*, now that you think of it, that Uncle Marten would move to an island where the chief thing that happened was that pilots crashed their planes there? Doesn't that seem a little *odd* to you when his own brothers were pilots? Doesn't that sound like it might be wishful thinking? Doesn't that say something about him?"

"Like what?" she asked. Sometimes it was like talking to a bowl of vanilla ice cream.

"Well, I don't know. Like maybe he *liked* the idea of pilots crashing."

"Why would he like that?"

"Well, I don't know, Jocelyn. People like strange things," I said vaguely because I didn't know either.

"Don't be ridiculous. He already told us he bought the island because it was convenient and for sale. I'm sure the fact that pilots crashed on it was neither here nor there as far as he was concerned."

"And another thing I'd like to know is why Uncle

Marten keeps filling up the house with Christmas crap!"

"There's that word again," said Jocelyn.

I was suddenly overcome with curiosity for the first time since the accident. And Jocelyn didn't seem to care at all. Sometimes I had the almost irresistible urge to take a crowbar and pry open the closed doors to her brain. "Well, *think* about it, Jocelyn. Why do you *think* he would do such a thing?"

"What are we speaking about now—buying the island or decorating the house?" she asked imperturbably, lifting her teacup off the little side table and taking a sip.

"Take . . . your . . . pick!" I said.

"I dunno," said Jocelyn, looking into the fire as if it were all the same to her, which I'm sure it was. She looked sad again. She always looked sad or absent or annoyed. But there was never, ever any spark. I wondered if there had been any before the accident. It was hard to like someone who was like a pile of wet logs that never caught fire. Had anyone ever liked her? Had her parents? Perhaps they looked on her as she grew up and *wished* they could like her. I imagined them locking their bedroom door at night and whispering to each other, "Do you like her yet?" "No, do *you*?" "No. Do you think we ever will?" "All our friends seem to like their children." "At least nominally." "You're *supposed* to like your children." "Are we beasts?" "I blame Jocelyn." "She *did* turn out to be such a wet dishrag, didn't she?" "Let's not let on to anyone that we don't like her." "God no, then no one will take her off our hands." "We'll be stuck with her forever." "Let's pretend she's got some likable qualities." "And send her to college in Australia."

I found such thoughts comforting as I sat in the chair sniggering to myself.

"Maybe he's just goofy about the holidays," suggested Jocelyn, taking another sip of tea languidly, ignoring my sniggers.

"Well, Canadian Thanksgiving came, and you didn't see any turkeys around or Pilgrim decorations."

"People don't really decorate for Thanksgiving the way they do for Christmas."

"They hang Indian corn."

"Oh well. Indian corn."

"That's not an argument. You can say, 'Oh well, Indian corn,' about anything. It doesn't mean anything. It just sounds like it does."

"I mean people don't get excited about Thanksgiving the way they do about Christmas. You don't see year-round Thanksgiving stores like you do Christmas stores. People don't start getting ready for Thanksgiving in July the way they do making things and shopping in July for Christmas. My mother's guild made decorations all year. They had craft fairs in September. Christmas is a bigger holiday because it's baby Jesus' birthday."

When she said that, "baby Jesus' birthday," I was afraid that the gulf between us was too huge to bridge and I stared into the fire. Christmas was so full of family tradition, I didn't understand people who wanted to make it all about the baby Jesus. Wasn't your family just as important to you as the baby Jesus? I'm sure he wouldn't have thanked you for it. The last time I looked, the baby Jesus had his own family and traditions, and I don't think one of them was Christmas. My parents never went to church, so I don't know if they believed in Jesus or not. It wasn't a hot topic in our house, and I could tell this was going to be an eyebrow raiser for Jocelyn.

The week before Christmas my mother would make little almond sprinkle cookies which we didn't have the rest of the year and which my mother would, in the spirit of the season, refrain from eating all herself because these were *Christmas* cookies, and my father would insist on getting a live tree that we could plant in the forest again afterward and visit in the summer, although every summer when we returned to the forest to check on our tree it was always dead, and my father always walked away scratching his head, with my mother begging him to save the earth another way and instead have an artificial silver tree. But we always had a live one again in the end. The argument about this became a cherished tradition in itself. We hung felt stockings we had decorated together when I was in kindergarten, and my mother insisted on telling me stories from all the traditions, Jewish and African and Tibetan and Buddhist and Hindu, and I sat patiently waiting for the part about Santa Claus. Christmas was my holiday, and what was sacred about it was my family, and when Jocelyn said "baby Jesus' birthday" like that should be the important part for good people, I wanted to throttle her. It was smug. As if she were part of some big club where all the members were privy to information the rest of us, crying in the wilderness, were not. As if anything were certain. Like her certainty in itself were virtuous. If there was one thing I thought she would have learned by now, it was that you cannot be certain. Baby Jesus had grown up and gotten himself killed. My parents had followed suit. So had Jocelyn's. Christmas was gone. But I didn't say anything. Instead I got up and went to bed. Over the stair railing as I went to my room I saw Humdinger watching Jocelyn from the kitchen doorway and, as I reached my door, pad silently over to her and offer her a mint.

JOCELYN

THE DAYS AND NIGHTS grew darker and wetter, but it didn't deter Meline.

"You're crazy," I said when Meline appeared, as she did—regular as clockwork—at my bedside at 2 a.m.

"Come on, come on, you always say that. Get dressed," said Meline impatiently. She was not at her best at 2 a.m. either, I noted, although I don't think she ever would have admitted it.

I sighed. There was no sense arguing. It was like arguing with a tornado. "My coat is still damp," I said when we reached the mudroom. "And my boots are still wet on the inside. They never get a chance to dry out."

"What do you do, step in creeks?"

"Your boots are wet, too," I pointed out, but Meline shoved her feet in them, ignoring me. She got herself worked up into a *state* for the search at this hour and I half expected her to start bouncing unseeing, unfeeling, off trees.

It was always a shock to leave the house at that time. The cold damp hit us as soon as we opened the door, and it was hard for me not to just turn around and go back to my warm bed.

The woods were full of fog patches. Occasionally we would see the red gleam of animal eyes, deer, raccoons, squirrels. Every time the flashlight picked up red eyes, I shrieked. At this hour all I could imagine was bears and cougars and maybe even, secretly, werewolves. We stayed out until the darkness began to lighten imperceptibly, and then we gave up and went back in.

"I'm telling you," I said one night at 3 a.m. It wasn't pouring for a change, but the mist clung to my hair in little beaded droplets, as uncomfortably wet as rain. "There's no hope. I can't keep this up. I'm mildewing."

"Nonsense, best thing for your skin. You'll never age."

I thought about not aging and was filled with horror. I did not want to be this age forever. I couldn't wait for time to carry me out of it. Away from it. Anything was better than this. But away to what? I couldn't imagine. That's when I felt like a deer in the headlights. There was nowhere to go. *Nowhere.*

We entered the woods and I prepared myself for another long, fruitless trudge, but this time the flashlight picked up something red and shiny. At first, thinking it was an animal's eyes, I turned to run out of the woods, but Meline stopped me, grabbing my arm. She pulled back the bush. Underneath it was a badly rusted aileron. "I think it's still usable." She squatted down, trying to pull twigs off it, while I held the flashlight steady. "It's got a lot of nicks and holes, but we should be able to patch those. Let's see if we can drag it back to the barn."

We grabbed an end together and between the two of us worked it out of the bushes. In the process, I cut my fingers and Meline banged it against her legs, ripping her pants in two places, but after that we were able to begin to pull it out of the woods and across the meadow.

"This means that Uncle's story was true," spluttered Meline excitedly. There was a little line of drool down her chin. Was she foaming at the mouth, finally? I had half expected her to come to that eventually. "There must be lots more parts. We're going to build a plane, Jocelyn."

"We won't be able to drag a fuselage or a cockpit," I said, huffing and puffing and trying to shift the metal to keep it from digging into the wounds on my hands. My mother had always told me that a lady was known by her hands. My mother's hands were rough with work, but she poured gallons of Jergens lotion on them every night and used an orange stick on her cuticles. "Or a whole wing. We can't drag that."

"That's why we need some kind of dolly. Remember I told you that at the beginning. When I first had the idea." Meline was shaking with excitement, but I felt no different. I looked at the plane part and tried to imagine what she was feeling. It was a plane part, that's all. We were building a plane. It didn't change anything. "I said that if we ever found the parts, we'd need a way to wheel the big pieces in. I'm glad we found this first, aren't you? Wouldn't it be frustrating to have to leave it in the bushes?"

"It's only one part," I said looking down at it, again trying to feel what it was that was getting Meline so animated, but I couldn't.

"Come on, the barn isn't that far from the house," said Meline in encouraging tones.

"I hope no one sees us. Humdinger's light is often on at night. He prowls."

"Well, no one's light is on now. I can see the house from here and it's dark."

Meline sat down for a second to rest. She was panting.

"Let's go," I said, suddenly tired of the whole business. I didn't care if we found any more parts. It was all so meaningless. "The sooner we get it into the barn, the sooner we can get to bed."

Meline heaved herself up and looked dizzy.

"What's the matter?" I asked.

"I just had a head rush, never mind," she said.

Then I realized it wasn't drool on her chin. Her nose was running right down her face. She must be getting a cold.

After we had deposited the aileron in the barn and stumbled back to the house, Meline threw her muddy clothes on the mudroom floor and, leaving them there, went up to bed without another word. I sighed and picked up my own and Meline's clothes and hid them behind the freezer as we always did before going upstairs. I could hear Meline coughing the rest of the night.

"I told her we'd get pneumonia," I said to myself as I fell asleep. "Mummy would never have approved of any of this." I dreamed of my mother again and it was always the same dream: my mother was coming out of the wreck of the train. Burnt up and bloodied bodies were everywhere and people crying and screaming, but my mother was always fine, unscathed and wearing her favorite sandy-colored light chiffon party dress, the one she had admired and wouldn't buy because it was expensive and impractical. I told my father about it and we gave it to her for Christmas. My mother loved the color. My father said it was the exact color of my hair and when my mother spun around it looked like my hair blowing in a breeze. My mother laughed and said, Don't be so fanciful, but it was always her favorite dress after that.

Now in the dream my mother looked beautiful and calm and comforting, and she drifted toward me, smiling gently. Just before she got to me, I always woke up. But I didn't wake up into consciousness, I woke up into another dream, only in this one my mother wasn't all right, she was dead and buried, and then, oh horror, when I went to tell my father I saw he was buried, too, and I had no one to tell, I was alone with this horrible information and I saw his grave and always said the same thing, "At least in my dream I got to see my mother once more before it happens. Why can't I see my father, too? Why?" And no matter what else happened in that second dream, this sat like a stone upon my heart, immovable, unchangeable. It was cruel, my subconscious. Why did it come to hurt me in the worst way night after night after night? Why did I dream such things? It pounded my heart into a flinty shield. I would feel no more. Not until night came again and the dream. And as soon as I saw my mother, my heart opened without a thought, and I was filled with joy and love for her, and then it happened again, just as it had in real life, and it would be as fresh and terrible as the first time, and I quivered with the shock.

I didn't want to go to sleep after that. But I was so tired during the day. Meline wore me out so with her energy and busyness. She pushed me to keep moving. She kept saying what else did I have to do? What else was I doing? How could I be tired, I never did anything. She didn't see how hard I had to work just to find a livable place inside myself. Always wanting to sleep during the day and always wanting to stay awake at night and avoid the dream. There was nowhere for me to live comfortably anymore. And I didn't know how to cope with any of this except by being polite. My mother said no matter what happened, a lady was always polite.

In the morning Meline coughed all through her breakfast. We were in the habit of going into the kitchen ourselves and making our own breakfasts now that we went to bed and arose so late. Uncle Marten had instructed Mrs. Mendelbaum to put breakfast out, a good hot English buffet breakfast, probably like the kind he had read about in novels, but after weeks of putting these dishes out on the buffet at seven and at ten taking uneaten serving dishes of eggs and toast and bacon and kidneys and fruit off the buffet and throwing them away, Mrs. Mendelbaum had had enough. "Vaste! All I see is vaste! ME KEN BRECHEN!" she said. "Enough." And she stopped putting breakfast out. We didn't care. We didn't want the big buffet breakfasts. I liked making my own toast and I think Meline did, too. That's what I did at home, and anything homelike was comforting, no matter how small. The grandness of Uncle Marten's house, the strangeness of the formal meals at the big table, had been just more newness that wore on the heart. I liked to have my toast alone in my room. Meline liked to sit in one of the cranberry-and-green wing chairs in front of the fire. Sometimes the cat came down and rubbed herself on my ankles while I was making my toast. Her warm purring quiet soft body was comforting.

The morning after finding the aileron, Meline was sitting in the wing chair by the fire eating Cheerios. The cat was padding around her chair. Meline kept coughing and spewing Cheerios everywhere. She cleaned up after herself each time, but watching from the kitchen doorway, waiting for my bread to toast, I found it stomach-churning. Couldn't she keep herself from spitting like that? "Disgusting," I said as Meline coughed and sprayed milk onto the tiling in front of the fireplace and the cat licked it up.

"She appears to have a cough," said Humdinger, who had come noiselessly into the kitchen, startling me. "I'm making breakfast for Mrs. Mendelbaum and taking it to her. She has the flu," he said in apologetic tones, I guess because he realized he'd startled me.

"I think Meline must have it, too," I said shyly. I had never spoken to Humdinger before. He had drifted about as a silent presence, not even staying long enough to be thanked when he gave me a mint.

"She ought to go to bed," said Humdinger, peering out the door with concern at Meline, who had started coughing again. "You don't mess around with the flu."

"No, I suppose not," I agreed. I remembered stories my mother told me of hundreds of people dying in flu epidemics.

"I had an aunt who died of the flu," said Humdinger,

as if reading my mind. "Of course, she was very old and in a weakened state."

"That's terrible," I said automatically but thinking, Hadn't we heard enough of death? Why did everyone have to keep mentioning death all the time?

To be fair, maybe it only seemed like everyone was mentioning death all the time because it was always on my mind, but I was in no mood to be fair. I was still mad about my dream. It seemed the universe was watching me with a malevolent eye and making endless trouble. I was mad at the universe and its evil, wily ways. This was not how I was raised to live. If you lived a solid, uncomplaining, productive life the universe was supposed to leave you alone. You were supposed to have, at the very least, a long trouble-free life. I was only sixteen. What had I done to deserve this? Nothing, I was sure. It was against all rules.

"Well," said Humdinger, placing the plate of muffins and the soft-boiled eggs he had made for Mrs. Mendelbaum on a tray, "you ought to tell her to go to bed. Get herself a good book and a nice pot of tea, that's my advice. And stay in bed until it passes." And he glided from the room like the wind.

"Right," I thought skeptically, because I knew what Meline's plans for the day were always like and they did not involve tea.

I took my toast and hot chocolate and was almost at my bedroom door when Meline called up to me, "Hurry and get dressed."

I stopped and looked down over the banister at Meline. "Mrs. Mendelbaum has the flu. Humdinger's aunt died of the flu."

"Well, I certainly hope Mrs. Mendelbaum doesn't die. I can't cook, can you?"

"No."

"Humdinger looks like he might."

"You can't be as unfeeling as you pretend," I said before remembering that unfeeling was exactly what I aspired to be.

"There's nothing unfeeling about it. I don't even know Mrs. Mendelbaum. You're the one who compared her to some dead aunt of Humdinger's. I'm just facing facts. If she dies, someone else around here will have to cook, at least until we can hire a new cook. Anyhow, hurry up and eat."

I looked blankly at Meline. Was she callous or was she mean? Could she really talk about someone dying so casually? I didn't think I would ever understand her. All she seemed to care about was building the plane. "I don't think you should be going out today. It's pouring rain. We didn't get any sleep and you're coughing."

"Who cares?"

"If you're going to ignore your health, then make sure you leave detailed instructions for me in case something happens to you, because I don't know how to put planes together." Let's see who's callous now, I thought, but she ignored this.

"I'm telling you, easy-peasy once you know what you're doing," she said. "Really, most of the things that grownups do don't take rocket scientists. If they did, most grownups wouldn't be able to do them either. It's just a matter of learning. But that's the problem for people. That's where they get stuck. They just assume they can't do certain things. They say to themselves, I'm only sixteen, I will have to wait until the magic age of twenty-five before I will be able to build a plane. But, of course, that's nonsense. Your brain doesn't get any smarter in those nine years. You could build a plane at the age of nine if someone would just show you how. And if you just believed you could and tried it. But it's just as well that people think like this, that sixteen-year-olds can't build planes, because then no one will ever guess that that's what we're doing and they'll leave us alone."

"Yes, leave us alone," I echoed, wondering how much more alone we could possibly be.

MELINE

"GET DRESSED!" I barked again at Jocelyn. Her eyes had gone back to someplace where she looked as if she were walking into a closet that went into another dimension. When she did that, it gave me the willies and I barked at her because it scared me to think she could go off like that and I was the only one seeing it. That the only thing keeping her from disappearing was me ordering her not to.

Jocelyn put on layers of shirts and sweaters because downstairs her coat was still soaking from the night before.

"What are we going to do for coats?" she said to me, looking like the abominable snowman as she came downstairs. "Peel off layers as they get drenched? The weight alone will pin us to the ground."

"Let's take these two," I said, pulling two rain parkas randomly off hooks in the mudroom. "No one will notice they're gone."

"We can't," said Jocelyn in horrified tones. "They aren't ours."

"They're bone-dry, though," I said. "You don't want to get pneumonia, too, do you?"

Jocelyn threw one on hastily and we went across the meadow, Jocelyn moving like a crab in a half scurry, looking back over her shoulder, afraid that the jacket owner would see us, I guess. It was only when we got to the cover of the woods that she slowed down. We moved logs and investigated mounds until we were exhausted and exasperated and wet through despite the parkas. I lay down on the ground under some trees and stared up into the gray clouds. I kind of liked being this tired. It made quitting for the day easier.

"Get up," said Jocelyn. "You can't lie in the muck like that. You're ruining someone's jacket."

"It'll wash," I began and then gasped and pointed overhead. We had never thought to look in the maze of branches overhead, but wedged in a treetop was the nose of a plane. We were on a roll.

Jocelyn gasped, too, and ran for the house. I followed her. By the time I had gotten in and hidden all my wet things behind the freezer, Jocelyn was already changed into dry clothes.

"What happened to you?" I asked, collapsing on the wing chair opposite her.

"I don't know," she whispered, sitting by the fire with a book and refusing to look up. "I was unnerved. Seeing it that way. Stuck up there all those years. The way it was in the treetop, it just seemed more crashed than the other plane, and then I thought some pilot died up there probably. In that treetop. It seemed so grotesque. So much more grotesque than dying on the ground. It seemed deader."

I went upstairs to take a bath. You can never tell how anyone is going to react to anything.

From the top of the stairs I saw Humdinger creeping up to the fire, offering Jocelyn a mint.

MARTEN KNOCKERS

"Oooo, more plum-colored ephemera," I cried, getting up from my chair and rubbing my hands together, gleefully anticipating unwrapping the big sodden box that Humdinger brought into my office.

"By the way, Humdinger, have you seen my rain parka? Every time I look for it, it's gone."

"Do you only have one?"

"Hmm, yes. Doesn't seem likely I would need two. Or it didn't before it started to disappear. I don't know what to do about missing things."

"Perhaps you should have a spare."

"Perhaps we all should. How many rain parkas do the girls have?"

"I believe they just have their winter coats."

"Yes?"

"Wool."

"Odd choice. No rain parkas?"

"I've never seen them wear any. Of their own."

"Then I'll order everyone some. How many do you think? Three apiece? If things are going missing, then three seems safe. Better make it four. And four for you and Mrs. Mendelbaum, too, I suppose. Don't want you dripping on the carpets."

"Thank you, but I have a rain parka and I suspect I won't need another when the girls get theirs."

What in the world did he mean? Most mysterious fellow, Humdinger. "I have no idea what you're talking about, but watch for Sam to drop them, will you?"

"Of course, sir."

"Ahem, well . . ." It hardly seemed like the time to ask Humdinger not to call me sir. The truth was, Humdinger didn't irritate me nearly as much as Mrs. Mendelbaum did. I hated being called sir but didn't want to embarrass Humdinger. You *couldn't* embarrass Mrs. Mendelbaum.

"I just saw the helicopter drop this box and so was able to rescue it before it became too sodden or got trampled by the bull. But it's almost time for dinner; perhaps you'd rather wait."

"Not at all, we're all eating too much anyway," I said with sudden inspiration. "I'm getting fat." I had put on a considerable pot belly since giving up my diet of hot dogs and mac and cheese. It turned out that one could develop quite an appetite given a certain variety in one's diet. It surprised me. Even though I ate absentmindedly, at some level I did indeed seem to be enjoying my meals more. I knew this because I caught myself sneaking down for more midnight snacks and going after the last little breast of veal nugget and a hunk of whatever cake Mrs. Mendelbaum had been mucking about with that day. I would probably swell to the size of a boulder and have to be rolled to conferences. But a box! Another Christmas box! I couldn't be happier. I really couldn't! I ran my hands through the two rows of curly hair that stuck up on either side of my bald pate, pushing aside my papers, motioning for Humdinger to bring the box over. What could it be? Something good, no doubt.

MELINE

BOXES ARRIVED REGULARLY and Humdinger would bring them in. We were finishing dinner when the rain parkas arrived. Jocelyn put her knife and fork down politely, and I started to cough again. I hadn't felt like eating for a couple of days. Jocelyn kept trying to get me to go to bed, but I told her we should get the airplane nose out of the tree and into the barn before I let myself be sick. We should have at least two pieces of plane before we took a break. Three would be better, but two at the very least.

"You can't *let* yourself be sick, you just *are* sick," Jocelyn had said as I coughed and clutched my ribs. I had not told anyone yet that I was having sharp pains in my ribs because it frightened me, and somehow telling people would make it more real and therefore more frightening.

Humdinger hesitated as usual to put the muddy box on the table. I guess, since he had started doing the laundry and the boxes had started arriving, he was spending a lot of unnecessary time washing tablecloths, but this was not the type of thing that would have occurred to Uncle Marten.

"Don't stand on ceremony, put it down, put it down," said Uncle Marten. Then he opened it with his steak knife and began to pull out rain parka after rain parka. He tossed four each to Jocelyn and me. We looked at each other and the same thought crossed both our minds: How much did they know?

"Do you mind if I take a tray up now to Mrs. Mendelbaum?" asked Humdinger, who had been watching our reactions to the rain parkas.

"Mendelbaum? Oh, yes, yes, yes, yes. Well, if Mrs. Mendelbaum's in bed ill, then who's been making dinner?"

"I have," said Humdinger. "I hope it has sufficed."

"Well, we're none of us starving, you can see that, can't you? But yes, very nice indeed. It's an amazing thing, a man who can cook. And find boxes! Oh, perhaps you'd find one who could do one. Or the other. But both? What are the odds? And if it were up to me we'd all be having mac and cheese. Well, in fact, it was up to me and we did have mac and cheese.

"But I could never do anything like this complicated business you keep serving for dessert that the girls seem to like so much," said Uncle as Humdinger brought in a bowl for each of us. "What is this stuff anyway? And how do you get the top all like that?"

"Crème brûlée," said Jocelyn, her face twitching with, I could see, the effort to force her eyebrows back down where they belonged. "Humdinger takes a kind of blowtorch to the top of the custard."

"Lots of imagination that," said Uncle Marten. "I, myself, would never think of taking a blowtorch *deliberately* to the top of a dessert. That it would result in anything nice. Might do it accidentally. Many great discoveries were accidents, of course. Although it's hard to imagine the kind of accident involving any dinner course and a blowtorch. So to do it on purpose, suspecting good things would result, acting on a *hunch* . . . well, it seems to me it takes a kind of genius."

"I used a recipe, actually," said Humdinger.

"Right. Well, it was still a *very* good idea," muttered Uncle Marten, who was drifting off, his crème brûlée spoon stuck in his mouth, as he pawed through the rest of the contents of the box. Humdinger slipped out.

"How can he say 'It's an amazing thing, a man who can cook'?" Jocelyn whispered to me, but my head had fallen on the table and it was too heavy to lift again. I'd been feeling hot and sleepy during dinner but now, ridiculous, felt suddenly much worse. "He can't be *that* out of touch."

I wanted to say something sarcastic about Uncle and not knowing men could cook, but I couldn't think of anything. Instead, to my surprise what came out was, "I think I have rocks in my head." I don't think anyone heard me, I was too far down at the end of the table. I wondered if I would lie there forever. All in all, it didn't seem such a bad prospect.

"Well, well, you look all done in, you pair, what say I just take my little treatsies with me?" And Uncle Marten swept up the other things that had come in the parka box and walked upstairs muttering away.

"It's dark out, less go," I said. It was difficult to speak articulately with my mouth pressed against the table by the weight of my suddenly too-heavy head. I noticed I seemed to have a little pool of drool forming under my right cheek. It was itchy but oddly comforting.

"It's too early to go out, and besides, you can't go out. You've gone beyond being a little sick." Jocelyn got up and put a hand against my forehead. "You've got a *fever*," she said accusingly. Not Florence Nightingale.

"Obvious," I said. So sleepy but have to explain. Jocelyn not smart. Can't put pieces together. "That's why so hot. But don't worry, drool cooling me off. Body is amazing thing. Gets too hot, sends drool."

"Well, you can't go out with a fever," said Jocelyn and pulled up a chair next to me. Sits down. Thinking about situation? Prim. Head still stuck to table. Ask for help? Doesn't seem in helpful mood.

"Can," say finally. Show spirit. Always rally in face of, what was in face of? Face of drool. Mustn't let Jocelyn get big ideas. Not idea person. Type ideas Jocelyn have? Ugh.

"I'm . . . telling . . ." said Jocelyn. Going to leave now. Guess. Bye, Jocelyn.

"Don't," call weakly after. Who going to tell anyway? All parents dead. No one to tattle *to*. Any other time, interesting question, but right now thing am going to die. *Think* am going to die. Join crowd. Jocelyn keep going. Want to call her bad name. Can't thing of any. *Think* of any. Always eating bread-and-butter sandwiches at four, that one. "Sandwich eater," call weakly. Best can do. Try not to be hard on self. Sick. Sudden sick. Whew. Didn't see comin'. Try not to be hard on self. Sick. Oh yeah, already said that. Said or thought? Thought. Doesn't matter. Nap would be good.

JOCELYN

I FOUND NO ONE in the kitchen and headed upstairs. I had no intention of telling Uncle Marten. He just wasn't practical. And Mrs. Mendelbaum was sick in bed and hadn't been seen for days. She would be no help. I would have to tell Humdinger. I *wanted* to tell Humdinger. I wanted to cry and tell Humdinger, and this made no sense to me. He looked like a corpse, he had feet like boats, he crept around offering mints at inappropriate times, and he was a Canadian, and yet, of everyone here, he was the one most likely to act in a rational manner, so

I marched up to his sitting room, where he was reading a paper and eating his dinner, and said, "Humdinger, I think there's something wrong with Meline. She has a fever. I think she may need medicine. And a doctor. She's really *much too hot!*" And then to my great embarrassment I burst into tears and couldn't stop the flow.

Humdinger didn't waste words or give my tears a second look but got up from the table, his napkin still stuck in his collar, and went downstairs to the dining room, where he found Meline, who had somehow managed to unstick her cheek, blissfully passed out on the floor, looking very peaceful. I trailed behind him as he carried her upstairs, deposited her on her bed, and then found Uncle Marten.

"One of the girls needs a doctor," he said, without knocking or his usual polite preamble.

"Which one?" asked Uncle Marten distractedly from his books.

"Meline."

"Well, we must get her one. You know where the phone book is, and the helicopter service number? Here, let's see, Sam." Marten Knockers wrote Sam's name and phone number on a Post-it and handed it and the radio phone to Humdinger. Humdinger nodded. "Call the hospital in Vancouver and tell whichever doctor they send to come supplied with medicine in case she needs it. What do you think she has?"

"She has a cough and fever."

"Antibiotics, most likely. Tell them to bring antibiotics and Tylenol. And whatever they think she might require that we don't have. Tell them we'll make a large hospital donation. Or whatever they want. Do we have any chicken soup about? I was just reading not long ago that that's not the old wives' tale they used to think. It really works."

"We have chickens in the freezer. I'll make some."

"You're an amazing creature, Humdinger. Blowtorches and chicken soup. Well, off you go. Let me know as things unfold. I'm sure it's nothing. People are always getting terrible fevers that turn out to be nothing. But how in the world could she have caught something on the island? No one lives here. Of course, Mendelbaum managed it. Very resourceful of her."

Humdinger moved swiftly and in no time a doctor was dropped off in the dark. Humdinger ran outside from where she dangled from the helicopter ladder.

"You put me down," the doctor yelled to Sam, shaking her fist, but Humdinger grabbed the ladder and held it steady for her so she could get off.

"Well, this is certainly nuts," she said. "Where's the sick girl?"

"Come on inside," Humdinger said and swept her into the house and out of the rain and up immediately to Meline's room.

MELINE

I HEARD PEOPLE COME IN, and when I opened my eyes and saw a woman's face suddenly looming kindly over me, I thought it was my mother's and said, "ARSHK!" in that moment thinking all my hopes had materialized and my parents had never been dead after all. When the woman startled I saw it wasn't my mother at all and thought how lucky I was to be on the island where I had fewer opportunities to see my mother's face in every kind stranger that came my way. Then I realized "arshk" didn't mean anything, and although I was thinking a little more clearly since my nap, I was still hot and cold and mixed up.

"I'm Dr. Houseman, Meline," she said. I closed my eyes for the rest of the exam and she began methodically poking me and pressing her stethoscope on me and I tried not to mind. They thought I was weak with illness, but I was trying to figure out how to put together the nose of one plane with an aileron from another. But I kept seeing it like a cartoon movie, the parts of airplanes rearranging themselves and forming new and strange machines.

"Meline, can you hear me?" asked Dr. Houseman more loudly than necessary and yet, oddly, it did sound as if her voice was coming from down a tunnel, a long way away. I nodded. "I don't know for sure and I can't be sure without a chest X-ray, but it sounds as if you have pneumonia."

I opened my eyes and just looked at her. I wondered if you could get it from being constantly warned about it. When I didn't say anything Dr. Houseman turned to Humdinger and said, "I'd feel better if you'd let me take her back to the hospital."

At this I sat bolt upright and said, "NO. NO hospital. NO."

"Now, now," said the doctor and then turned to Humdinger again. "So her parents are?"

"Dead," said Jocelyn, who was lurking in the doorway. "She lost them both a few months ago."

"I'm sorry," said Dr. Houseman.

"Mine died, too," said Jocelyn, which seemed to me to be extraneous attention-seeking information, and if it occurred to the doctor she only repeated "I'm sorry," and then turned to Humdinger yet again.

"Well, I've heard worse chests but I've heard better. If she won't go to a hospital I want you to watch her, don't let her leave the bed, lots of fluids, make sure she takes the full course of antibiotics I'm going to leave for her, and if the fever spikes I don't care what she says, you bring her in."

"Right," said Humdinger. "Anything else?"

"This is a very strange place to live," said Dr. Houseman, seemingly taking note of her surroundings for the first time and looking around my massive bedroom with its four-poster bed and high arched wood-carved ceiling. I could see her point. "You know the air force used to crash planes here? There was some kind of a scandal—some captain or something gone mad who was sending all these young men to their deaths for no reason."

"Corps of the Bare-Boned Plane," I said.

"She's not delirious, that's what they called it," said Jocelyn.

"Huh!" said Dr. Houseman, considering. There was a pause, and I wondered if she'd left, so I opened my eyes and there she still stood. She had a large beaklike nose and a careworn face, dark eyes with deep crinkles at the corners, probably from squinting when she tried to see deeply into wounds, and an air of resolute calm, the air of someone who has learned to be this way after a lifetime of being exasperated with the type of things she had to see. Her hair was streaked randomly with gray as if a child had done it with a paintbrush. She wasn't pretty. I'm not sure if she was even handsome, but she did have likable features. She looked like someone you'd never have to save. She was thin and looked strong, as if she was used to doing all her own lifting. I had the feeling doctoring had been her whole lonely life. You could tell she was one of those earnest people with a purpose that makes them kind of weary and tired in middle age from being always the only serious one in a roomful of people who took life a little easier. As if she knew this made her different and strange and loneliness went with it and it might not have been what she'd have chosen.

"It would be so much easier if before we were born we could pick our temperaments. So we didn't get stuck with one that made us unhappy," I said, completing my long reverie aloud.

Everyone looked down at me with worried expressions and I began to get a sense of what it must be like to be Uncle Marten.

"Don't you think?" I asked and then fell asleep again.

I lay bedridden, in the worst of my illness, beyond reading or chatting or directing traffic. Unable to do anything but take a few spoonfuls of the soup Humdinger kept bringing me, with Mrs. Mendelbaum on his heels snapping away, "I told you, stop making soup behind my back, ahzes ponim. A tall, goyishe cadaver cannot, can *not* a proper chicken soup make. I never heard of such a thing. Oy vey, get me a chicken, get me some shmaltz, get me an onion, get out of my way, all of you," she would say, running into my bedroom after him in her housecoat, her hair flying in six directions at once, her stockinged feet slipping on the floor, a knife in one hand and a chicken in the other. But Humdinger would just calmly take the knife and chicken back and suggest she go to bed. Suggesting people go to bed was becoming his little specialty. She was still very ill herself, said Jocelyn, and Dr. Houseman had prescribed bedrest and Tylenol. Then he'd settle down and make a perfectly reasonable chicken soup with the muttered outraged oaths of Mrs. Mendelbaum drifting down from the second floor.

Once she came downstairs and looked into the soup pot and yelled "WHAT? NO DILL? What kind of farkuckt soup is this? You cannot have chicken soup without dill." Mrs. Mendelbaum rolled up her sleeves and began to take the soup over to the sink to throw it out preparatory to starting over, but it was too heavy for her in her weakened state and she dropped the soup pot. I was downstairs getting a water bottle and watched in horror as the greasy soup flew all over the kitchen, flooding the floor and splashing the walls. Mrs. Mendelbaum screamed, and Humdinger pulled her swiftly out of the stream of hot liquid and, after determining that she hadn't been burned, escorted her back to bed with promises that he would make the soup to her exacting specifications. All of this I watched with some fascination, remembering how Humdinger had just finishing cleaning the kitchen before Mrs. Mendelbaum's arrival in it. He hadn't said any of the things I would have been tempted to. When he came back downstairs and began mopping up soup I said, "Do you really think you can't have chicken soup without dill? Who would notice?" I was trying to be sympathetic and apologetic for Mrs. Mendelbaum's behavior, since I figured someone in the household should come to his defense, but he said, "It doesn't matter. Mrs. Mendelbaum isn't happy and we're going to make it right for her."

MARTEN KNOCKERS

YOU WOULDN'T THINK it would be so difficult to keep sick people in their rooms, I thought as I watched Mrs. Mendelbaum yelling chicken soup directions over the banister. While Mrs. Mendelbaum and Meline lay ill, I was spending an inordinate amount of time online with my credit card, going from site to site, searching for deep plum and gold Christmas ephemera, napkins and pillows and tree skirts and tablecloths. Especially tablecloths, because Humdinger, who always had well-thought-out timely advice, had suggested a spare might be a good idea in case someone spilled something and rendered the new velvet one unusable. This would not occur to someone like me who never did laundry. In the old days, before Mrs. Mendelbaum, I would just wear my shirts until even I could smell them, and then throw them out. I always bought cheap ones because I did not want to be accused of conspicuous consumption. Even though it was my own money, to do with as I liked, and at that time there was no one to accuse me of anything.

Because Humdinger encouraged me to buy another tablecloth I ordered three more. On the same site, I ordered large golden angels with flowing blond hair and wreaths of gold filigree to hang on all the doors. These angels gave me more pleasure than anything; they represented something if only I could put my finger on it, some softness associated with virtue, not fire and brimstone but nurturing. I hadn't had any religious background or study myself, but the Catholics seemed to have captured something, and all those Italians with their Renaissance Madonnas. I liked the idea of some womanly figure hanging on the walls blessing the house for the holiday season. And then at the end of Christmas packing her into a box again and putting her in the attic. It seemed to me that women were better at this type of thing, this house-blessing thing, than men. But perhaps not. That Humdinger was good at making things run smoothly. Certainly better than Mrs. Mendelbaum. What you wanted was an air of calm confidence and a certain serenity. It was hard for me to believe than anyone was serene a good portion of the time, let alone all the time. I found it a most elusive state myself. I bought shiny golden prisms to hang from the already rococo chandeliers and Victorian lamps. The whole house was beginning to glow with the golden light I was purchasing for it. I filled the inside with the deep plums and the dark piney greens of the woods. The light sank into the velvets and bounced off the glittering sparkling decorations. And every night I saw Jocelyn leave the house, flashlight in hand. Leaving all this light I was creating and going into the dark pouring rain. It was really very odd behavior.

One night at dinner she wanted to know about animals on the island. "Well," I said, racking my brain because this wasn't something I paid much attention to. "Deer and raccoons, of course. Hmmm, what else? Ah!" I said, cutting into the perfectly grilled steaks that Humdinger had put before us, "Bulls! Or rather, a bull!" I remembered Humdinger had mentioned saving a Christmas box from a bull. And now that I thought of it, this was a very surprising thing for Humdinger to have said. "Am I remembering right? Did Humdinger say we had a *bull*? He must have been mistaken. He must have seen a largish squirrel."

The truth was that I was spending far more time these days buying Christmas things than I was working on negative density even though I pretended to myself otherwise. The way the Internet had a hold on me was that I would ponder infinite space for a few seconds and then put a call in to some company selling crystal icicles to hang on trees and then try to keep both things in my mind while I talked to the clerk, which made ordering things by phone take much longer, as the clerk had to separate the physics that crept into the ordering information. I very seldom found a clerk who could talk physics worth a darn. If I had just admitted to myself that it was more fun to order Christmas ornaments than it was to study negative density, the clerks and I might have been spared all this. But no, I kept revisiting the Internet every ten minutes. And I was having more and more trouble with negative density; I did not understand it, so it was becoming something of a bore. The problem, I finally decided, was not that I didn't understand negative density, it was that I didn't understand what *other* people had written about it. Then I had the pivotal revelation that everyone else was just absolutely wrong and I was just absolutely right. That, it turned out, was a principle that stood me in good stead. Oooo, but speaking of negative density, I said to myself, as I proceeded ahead with my own hypothesis, I wonder if Neiman Marcus has any plum or gold accessories in its online Christmas catalog? And the problem with negative density took a backseat again. My mind now went from the bull Humdinger said he saw to a set of very cute plum floor cushions and a hassock that I could use to replace my current leather one. The plum-colored one was tufted. "And I do so love tufts," I said.

"I wish I could have a dog," said Jocelyn. "Aren't bulls supposed to be afraid of dogs?"

"No, *tufts*, not dogs, tufted hassocks," I said.

"No, a *dog*," insisted Jocelyn. "You know, a greyhound or a basset hound or a bloodhound."

"Don't get stuck on hounds," I advised her.

Apparently Jocelyn told Humdinger that I said she could have a dog and Humdinger had Sam pick up a puppy from the SPCA. When the dog crate was lowered in a harness from Sam's helicopter a few days later, I, who was looking out my window and didn't remember anything about the conversation from dinner a few nights before, thought, Is that a dog coming onto the island?

Another creature? My God, why don't they just put up condominiums! It's too crowded here already. I swear to God I'm going to have to move myself if this keeps up. And I put my dresser in front of my door and forgot all about them until I got hungry and then couldn't find a way to get out of my room because I couldn't find the door and had forgotten that the dresser now stood in front of it. At the time, I thought my door had simply, inexplicably disappeared.

"What," I moaned plaintively, "is happening to all the doors in this house?" and I sat on my bed eating soda crackers in bewilderment all night from a box next to my bed. It's a good thing I keep crackers by my bed, I said to myself comfortingly. And then I couldn't remember for the life of me *why* I kept soda crackers there and, in fact, couldn't remember having put them there at all, and all I could think to offer to myself as explanation was that things around here were getting very strange in general. Very strange. I wished I had the cat to curl up with, but she had detected that her usual means of egress was no longer open to her and had gone out the window some time before. A full moon was shining in the sky, illuminating the fields, and I gazed out idly, searching for the rumored bull I kept forgetting to ask Humdinger about.

I saw Jocelyn out with a flashlight and the puppy. "Out and about at this hour? But *they* have doors in their rooms," I said, greatly disgruntled, and fell asleep, exhausted by my unsuccessful attempt to find a door.

JOCELYN

"THIS PUPPY THING is not going to work," I said out loud as I crossed the meadow with the puppy leaping around and straining at the leash. "I need a dog. I wonder how long it takes a puppy to turn into a dog? Probably too long for our purposes. Why did Humdinger get me a puppy? I asked for a dog." I was talking feverishly to myself. I had discovered that that was what I did when fearful. When I awoke and was alone in the train car, the car leaning on its side, the outside full of fire, I called for my mother and, when no one answered, started walking slowly down the empty train corridor. At some point I started talking to myself, gibbering away a mile a minute, things like "I do not know what I will find. I do not like this all the people are gone and there should be people why did no one come and get me what are those fires out the window they are probably not something very bad." I kept it up until I saw the first body parts, and after that I did not talk again for a very long time. Now I was in the dark again talking to myself, and I wondered if I would always be in the dark feverishly talking to myself from now on.

I had never liked being out at this hour, especially not alone. But Meline hadn't lifted her head or even awakened from her sick sleep any of the times I went into her room to peer anxiously at her. I had been hoping that if I spoke to Meline, she would beg me to wait until she was well enough to join me in the hunt for airplane parts, but for three days Meline had been so sick that it was apparent that she wouldn't be able to communicate with me at all for a while and that it was now up to me. I didn't really believe we would find all the airplane parts we needed, and didn't believe that even if we did, Meline could actually build a plane, but I needed that bit of hope and I needed to be convinced over and over. With Meline ill, I did not have this luxury. I had to believe on my own. And I wasn't sure I could. I didn't really understand why we were building the plane in the first place. Meline was so intent on it, she could make me believe in it, too. But without Meline, I wasn't sure what we were doing to begin with. Tonight, in the dark, it just seemed daft. And the puppy wasn't helping. *He* was supposed to be protecting *me*, but now I found myself worried that a bull would eat him. Did bulls eat small animals?

"I'm going to have to go farther afield, away from the house, and then what?" I said. Uncle might not believe in the bull, but Humdinger was more reliable than Uncle when it came to, well, almost anything. "I'll never find the airplane parts. But on the other hand, if I don't look, what will I do with my time? Alone, rattling around that house with nothing but my thoughts. What will I do at night except dream?" The puppy gave a great tug on the leash. I lost my grip and it raced off. "Oh no. Is it chasing something? Would a puppy be stupid enough to chase a bull? Probably. This on top of everything else. Now I won't be able to go back until I find the puppy. I can't leave a puppy out in the rain. And a puppy is going to be even harder to find than airplane parts because it doesn't reflect light. I haven't even named it yet. If I call 'puppy,' will it come? Why should it? I'm not the one who feeds it. It will run off and get gored. And why do bulls have to go around goring everything? What kind of life is that, to be born wanting to snort and ram everything with your horns? No wonder there are bullfights. As far as I am concerned, that is the bull's fault."

I walked on, straining to hear any sound at all over the rain. "And now I won't know whether a sound I hear is a bull in the bushes or a puppy. I can't run from rustling sounds either in case it *is* the puppy. This is precisely why you should never take on the care of a small defenseless animal. What I really had in mind was a large, mean Doberman. Why did I think I wanted a hound? What good would a hound do in an emergency? Howl the bull to death? But even a hound makes more sense than a puppy. It was very ill thought out on Humdinger's part. I would go back and tell him right now except I'm soaking wet and—" I cried out. My flashlight picked up the gleam of something in the bush and my first thought was that it was two staring bull's eyes. "Bull's eyes, bull's-eyes." I fled back across the furrows, getting my feet caught in holes and falling over mounds, scrambling back up without even registering I had fallen. "Bull's-eyes, where had I seen them? Oh yes, target and archery classes. Targets are so hard to hit. They place them against hay bales. Hay bales would be sodden in this rain. Good thing Saskatchewan doesn't get rain like this, but I'll never live in Saskatchewan again. I hadn't thought of that before. I am *never* going home."

I stopped, as if this thought had activated brakes in my legs, and I stood with my mouth open in the pouring rain, tears flowing down. I was *never* going home. There was no home. I started running again, fleeing the thought, but my foot caught and I tripped and the wind was knocked out of me. Blissfully, I could think of nothing for several moments but getting my breath back. When I got it back and nothing came galloping out of the dark to gore me, I realized it hadn't been eyes I had seen. It was metal. I had run all the way across the field from the thing I was seeking.

MELINE

THE NEXT MORNING when Jocelyn knocked on my door I could see that she was relieved to find me awake. She dragged something into the room that was covered in an old ripped sheet.

"Look what I found," she said proudly.

I sat up excitedly. "I can't believe you found something on your own."

"Yes, of course I did," said Jocelyn, sounding irritated.

"Well, you shouldn't be dragging it inside where everyone is going to see it. Why didn't you just leave it in the barn?"

"Because I knew you'd want to know what it was and I don't know how to describe it." She took the sheet off.

"Oh," I said. I could see her problem. It was part of a horizontal stabilizer, but so twisted it was practically unrecognizable. "Well, put it in the barn and we'll see about straightening it out later. It's a stabilizer."

"I'm leaving it here. I'll take it out to the barn tonight. I just want to go to bed."

"You were out all night until you found this?" I asked because frankly this didn't sound much like Jocelyn. It was more her speed to go out for ten minutes, decide it was too wet, and come in for hot chocolate and cookies.

"I found this almost immediately. I spent nearly the rest of the night afterward looking for the darned puppy."

"Can we say 'darned' if we can't say 'crap'?" She looked at me with a stricken face but I was too ill to care. I did not want new friends. I did not want new beginnings.

MARTEN KNOCKERS

I PASSED JOCELYN looking like a drowned rat as usual. Well, if she would go out in the rain at all hours. She squinted at me with something like disdain when I spilled my tea. I was trying to walk down the hall with a cup of tea in one hand while reading a book with the other; periodically I would slosh tea and then stop and wipe it up with the corner of my dressing gown. But apparently she wasn't a girl who properly appreciated the multiple uses of a dressing gown. I had bought myself a deep plum velvet one and some carpet slippers and fancied I looked very distinguished and Victorian. I was practically a Christmas ornament myself! Every time I wiped up tea I'd ask, "What are all these scratch marks all over everything? There are grooves in the floor like someone was dragging something. Why would they do that? It's that Mendelbaum woman. Oooo, I must give her my list of Christmas goodies to bake." I marched immediately upstairs to Mrs. Mendelbaum's bedroom and knocked on her door.

"Loz mich tzu ru. Go away, I'm busy being sick," said Mrs. Mendelbaum.

"What in the world is that?" It looked as if she was happily drinking a bottle of shoe polish.

"My friend Sophie sends me six bottles of her cough

medicine when she sends my things. A secret recipe from the shtetl. So, does she think I am going to spend my days coughing? But she says all the women in the shtetl keep it so on their shelves. For emergencies. For their nerves. For childbirth. Who should have such nerves?"

"Really, I wouldn't if I were you, Mrs. Mendelbaum. You never know what's in these herbal doodads. Not regulated."

"I should cough myself into a coma? Go away, I am sick."

"Yes, I know you're sick *now*, Mrs. Mendelbaum, but you don't plan to be sick the week before Christmas, do you? When you *should* be cooking."

"How should I know?" asked Mrs. Mendelbaum. "Now I am sick. Later, who can say? Do you think this is sickness that I want? Who would want such a thing?"

"Oh dear," I said. You just never knew what was going to set her off. "I don't mean to inconvenience you, but you don't really mind cooking when you're sick, do you? I've bought a goose."

"A goose. You want me to cook a goose?"

"Well, it isn't very good raw, I would imagine."

"How do I know now whether or not I will be too sick to cook a goose when the time comes?"

"Well, you can't be sick forever, I mean, can you?"

"Az a yor ahf mir, Mr. Smarty Pants."

I really hated it when she called me Mr. Smarty Pants. It seemed to me that if someone was paying you for doing nothing but lying around being sick, the least you could do was not call him names.

"Well, you could, um, you could RALLY! That's what you could do, Mrs. Mendelbaum. People do rally. They rally all the time. They rally do. Hahaha. Or you could cook while sick. I suppose people must do that, too. Especially people who live alone. Otherwise they would all die, wouldn't they?"

"What? Cook when I'm sick? You should eat food cooked by a sick person? And for Christmas? Who knows from cooking geese? A nice chicken maybe and a few latkes."

"I don't even know what those are," I said briskly. "Anyhow, I've made a very careful list of just the right kind of Christmas foods. The goose, of course, we've already discussed that." Discussing the menu made me feel like the lord of the manor. Usually these days I felt completely out of control in my own house. It irked me. "Chestnut stuffing, sweet potatoes, Brussels sprouts amandine, a plum pudding, a trifle, and a bûche de noël. I'm not married to the Brussels sprouts amandine. You could do them up any way you like. With mint, for instance. There's someplace I've left you scope for imagination, Mrs. Mendelbaum, if that gives you any pleasure."

"Why should Brussels sprouts give me pleasure? Lying on a desert island having my toes sucked, that should give me pleasure, too, I suppose."

"Please, Mrs. Mendelbaum, let's try to focus on the menu," I said.

"These starlets, with their fancy-shmancy pedicures, so they should lie in the sand having their toes sucked. This is a life?"

"Please," I repeated. It seemed that not only would Mrs. Mendelbaum not cook, she wouldn't even talk about it.

"My friend Sophie sends me movie magazines. Such things to amuse me when I'm ill. Humdinger brings them to me. Go to a hospital, Zisel, she begs me."

"You're not thinking of leaving us, are you, Mrs. Mendelbaum?" I asked worriedly. "Before cooking Christmas dinner?"

"And what's all this about bushes? Making a bush? You want me to cook a bush? What kind of strange goyishe rite is this?" croaked Mrs. Mendelbaum, putting her hands to her ears, but appearing to talk more to herself than to me. "The waltzes have begun again in my ears. Oh, please go away. I hear Viennese waltzes again. Ach, go, go. A kabaret forshtelung in my head. Go."

"Poor woman is delirious," I said to myself, going out and closing the door and then, on second thought, sliding my menu under it. She could study it in her own time.

MRS. MENDELBAUM

AM I GOING CRAZY? I think I am better becoming, my
fever, it has gone, and just a bit of the cough left, and I
begin to see him, my Ansel, my gelibteh, and the café in
Vienna where we met. I do not mean I imagine such
things, that I see them in my mind's eye and my memory.
No, to me they become real. My bedroom becomes the
café and there I sit, young, stylish, in my new black skirt
and the black stockings with the clocks on them. Oh such
stockings, I have not had a pair like them since. Vienna
then was what, so full of intrigue. Such a place. Like over-
ripe fruit, it smells of things that are too much, too easily
gotten by some, the table full of fruit that rots because
the ones who are allowed it have more than even their appetites will allow for. It frightens my mother, I see, this
Vienna, but I am young, I am aware, but it does not seem
that anything could happen to the young like me.

And as I see the café again, so clearly, I begin to think
as I have not for so many years, in German again. It was
skating on thin ice to go to the café alone like this with
my cigarettes and coffee. There was talk that I would not
be allowed to do so much longer. That even if such a
thing were not declared, I might disappear and no one in
the police would bother to find out how. Like playing in
traffic, was what it was. After your mother had told you

not to. That's why it was so exciting, of course. But it wasn't really as exciting as it could have been because I wasn't pretty enough to be taken much notice of and I didn't dare wear the kind of makeup that would have made me more noticeable and my hair was all wrong. It still hung all the way down my back, and even if I put it up it didn't have the look of the sophisticated new perms. All it said about me was newly out of mama's house but not really a woman yet, not interesting, not even really that pretty. Just young and innocent, which attracted certain types, but I could always tell the types, they always approached as if their own black clouds of intentions pulsed like heartbeats beneath the surface, they were rotting in their own ways, and when I saw them coming, I quickly sent them on their way.

I should have stayed out of the cafés probably, but it was the only place where I could go to be alone. Our house was full of my sisters and brothers and family members who had escaped other places where Jews were being treated even worse. So much worse sometimes, according to the newly arrived, that we didn't know whether to believe their stories. There was a haze everywhere, elusive like smoke, of bad things that might happen to us. I was young and full of hope and didn't want to hear about these bad things, so when I had had enough I would put on all my finest things and come and sit in the café as if I could find the truth of a happier future for myself. I knew unsavory things were happening everywhere, not just to the Jews, even here in the back room of the café. No one made any attempt to hide them from a young innocent girl like me, no, I knew that they thought if I didn't want to see such things I should stay out of Viennese cafés. It was as if suddenly there was a license for those who did not have to worry about their futures to let loose their beasts, you could see them almost, their snarly bestial heads poking out of their chests, the other that they could be. Are we all like that, I wondered. If Father did not have to worry, would there be a beast in him, too? In me? If we knew we could have control of other people, would we use it? Why not? What, after all, would make us different?

I began to see that everywhere there was either the doomed surrender of the preyed upon or the strange ecstasy of those dark figures coming into power and the kind of madness that ensued as people tried forbidden fruits and more and more strangers knocked on my mother's door with stories of atrocities elsewhere. Everyone could feel tensions building. Bad things coming. "All we have left is sitzfleish," said my mother worriedly. Patience that can endure sitting. But I was very young and I preferred the ugliness of the predators to the kind of pessimism I was seeing at home with my own people. I was tired of it, everyone talking of escape but no one leaving. Why not then go out and have a good time? And more and more men were looking at me as standards loosened, slipped, as I came into the café time and again. What was

I offering them, they wondered. I could see I excited just enough curiosity by coming again and again, by sitting alone. Anything that elicited curiosity, that titillated in any way, hooked these men, for a small time at least. They won't look when, if my uncle is right, we are all treated differently as Jews. If, as he predicts, bad things are to happen. Then they will not see me at all. Then I will go from being unseen to not being at all and I am young, I have not yet been, and if I am not to be in the future, I will be now. I will not sit quietly afraid in the house when I have not yet had a life.

One dark November before the Christmas lights would brighten the gloomy streets again, just as I finished the dregs in my tiny china cup and stubbed out my cigarette, a man came in. He was small and neat and beautiful with bright eyes, and he was stopping for directions, but then he saw me, so he ordered coffee and sat at the bar drinking it and looking shyly at me—I have never seen eyes like that—until I signaled the waiter and ordered another cup, too, although it was time for me to go. And then I did something no lady should, I went boldly to the bar and invited this man to come sit at my table.

"Cousin! To find you here!" I said to the man because the waiter was eyeing us curiously. I had never been so bold.

"Ah, you remember me, your cousin Ansel, I thought you might not," he said, taking his coffee carefully to my table and pulling out my chair.

"Yes, but do you remember your cousin Zisel?" I asked.

"Of course, and I remember how you love cake," said Ansel and ordered pieces for both of us, sending the curious waiter away.

And as it was getting on into evening the small band came in and began, as they always did at this hour, before being replaced by raunchier acts, the waltzes, and the sound of waltzes tinkled out into the lights of the street, drawing in more and more people until the café filled but we didn't notice, my Ansel and I. Not that night or ever again so long as we were together. And the world slipped away bit by bit. Ansel took me from Vienna to Canada because he knew, too, that bad things would begin happening and it would soon be harder if not impossible to go. And he was not like my family. He would not just wait it out. My mother begged me to wait with the rest of them until they were sure, perhaps things would not be so bad, perhaps stories were exaggerated, this was their home, but Ansel was sure and I was sure of Ansel. And because my family would not go with us, Ansel and I left without them, and I thought over and over how I was the one who did not want to listen to the warnings but I was the one to go, and the rest of them, who talked of nothing else, stayed. But I must admit I thought little of them after I left. For me, the whole world had become Ansel.

When last I heard of my family, years after coming to Canada—because at the time there was never any word, too many had been displaced, lost, died, no one really knew, it was better to wait until news came to you, it was better not to spend too much time thinking: the possibilities were too many and too horrible—it was a friend of a distant cousin who would tell me definitely that they were all gone, all those in my household who had waited too long, put in camps, not even in the same camps mostly but spread out, far apart, to die. Some of the family members, this friend thought, had ended up together, but she couldn't tell me which ones. She had only heard rumors that some had been together. She had been at a camp herself but not with any family. Better that way, this woman thought. She longed for familiar faces but soon she saw it was better not to see those faces dying before you. It was lonely, yes, but better to imagine them with hope, she thought. Maybe not. Maybe to be together would be comfort to all. Maybe there was no better any which way. Oh well, for sure, Zisel, though, all gone. That she knew for sure. There were networks. People worked hard to pass on news. It was all they could do now. Did it do any good or just spread misery? Perhaps they were beyond all misery. Was there a point you got to beyond misery? She didn't know. But I could not speculate with her. I had left my family many years ago in more than one way and made my life with Ansel. And the family friend was only envious when she saw how little it affected me. It would be heaven to be so unaffected, she said. Ich zol azoy vissen fun tzores, she said, and moved on.

Even after I got this news I was too busy to think of them, my dead parents, my dead brothers and sisters. I had babies one after the other, such blessings, and we lived in a bubble together for many years, safe, it seemed, in Canada. Safe forever. This would be my life forever. It did not occur to me that this, too, would pass. There were no Nazis but there was still death. It was not only Nazis who separated families. One by one, they died. Ansel first, then my four boys, one by one, cancer, a car accident took two, and finally my Menachem, my kaddishel. As if everything that had happened to me from the café until his death had been a long and happy dream. The dream world had been the good one. What had I done with my time in those dream days? I had fed them all. It didn't seem much, but I knew now it was everything. It was everything my life. Soups and kreplach and matzo balls. All the things I had learned from my mother. The way to add the ingredients to make the dense honey cake substantial yet light. All the formulas for being the way I had learned to be. And yet, I knew who I became did not come from such recipes, it came from Ansel and our boys. But now there was no one to say, ah, only Zisel can make such a light honey cake, the way Ansel had always said it. His way of saying there was only me in the world for him just as for me there had only been him. No one anymore knew what I was making, let alone that only I could make it so. I had been who I was for so many years because I had been so in Ansel's eyes. It was not that I was wonderful and so he found me so. It was that because he found me wonderful, I was.

MARTEN KNOCKERS

"WHAT IS THIS, some kind of rat?" I asked Humdinger because the island was full of rats and now it appeared one was dripping on the carpet.

"No, that is a dog," said Humdinger in patient tones.

"What's he doing *here*?" I asked in astonishment. A dog, of all things. Were we starting a petting zoo?

"You told Jocelyn she could have a dog."

"I did? I *did*? Fancy that. But it isn't even Christmas."

"I don't believe it was a present exactly."

"Presents! You know, Humdinger, I've been so focused on Christmas accessories and paraphernalia that I completely forgot that people get *presents* for Christmas. This opens up a whole other catalog-ordering opportunity, now, doesn't it? I mean, I've never had anyone to buy presents *for*. Goodness, what do *you* want, for instance?"

"I couldn't say."

"But you *must*. You *must* say. I have no idea what a tall, middle-aged man might desire in the way of Christmas bounty. Do you like neckties? No, you wear that odd kind of collar thing, don't you? A butler collar, I guess it is. Never knew there was such a thing. So I guess butlers don't need neckties."

"Indeed, neckties are very nicely thought of as Christmas gifts."

"Yes, yes, yes, I suppose they are. Don't want any myself. Take that off my list immediately, if you please, Humdinger. Yes, well, how about chocolates? Women love the stuff. I hear butlers like to eat. Most of them are on the portly side, which is to say, fat. And it's been my observation that fat people love chocolate."

"Many people love chocolate, true."

"You know this is kind of like being in a musical duet with you, Humdinger, where you repeat or paraphrase the tag line of every stanza. I feel we should put this whole conversation to music. Do you sing, Humdinger?"

"Regrettably, no."

"Pity. Well, I suppose you don't have a sweet tooth either, eh, Humdinger? The old sweet tooth. The foil of many a butler."

"I wouldn't say sweets were my foil, no."

"Well, then perhaps some macadamia nuts. People tend to be either sweet or salty in their snacking preferences. The old chocolate or nuts choice, I call it. You know, I've been reading these Christmas gift catalogs and they do seem to sell an awful lot of macadamia nuts. Expensive. Unusual. Exotic. Hawaiian. But now me, Humdinger, I don't associate Hawaii with Christmas.

Leis, luaus, hula girls doesn't spell Christmas to me. What you want is snow and reindeer and mistletoe and a lot, really a *lot* of plum accessories. That's what you want. That and a Jesus or two in a stable."

"One is usually considered sufficient."

"Yes, but we've got money. Gobs. No use being sufficient when you can be excessive. We'll have two. That way no one will have to fight over them. Have you ever seen people fighting over a baby Jesus?"

"I can't say that I have." Humdinger started to roll his eyes but stopped. I must say I was surprised. I had never seen him roll his eyes before. It was most unlike him.

"Oh yes, bloodshed, I assure you. I'm looking back now down that long tunnel to my childhood."

"A lot of baby Jesus fights in your youth, were there?" asked Humdinger politely.

"Well, yes, as in the best of families, of course," I said. "Bloody things, as I say. My brothers and I would take turns stealing it and hiding it in soap dishes and such. Drove my mother crazy. This way, you see, if anyone feels like stealing it we have a spare for the crèche. Anyhow, one Jesus was clearly not enough. They dispensed with him quickly enough, now didn't they? Of course, you've got to be crazy to volunteer for that job anyway, don't you? I mean really. Lamb of God, ha. Lamb chops. That's what they do with lamb. Ever been around during lambing season, Humdinger? All those wonderful lambs running in the field, spring's miracle, life renewed. Well, they don't just send them all to Club Med, now do they? So sad and yet so tasty, that should be mankind's motto. *Ha!* I don't consider myself a religious man, Humdinger, but everyone knows the story whether you believe it or not. That whole mess at the end with nailing people up on crosses. Of course, Romans were doing that all the time. Regular weekend entertainment, like going to the movies. You know, I think it would make a good paper that, things people do to entertain themselves on the weekend. I mean that in the larger sense, of course. Weekend metaphorically, yes . . ."

I whipped out a notebook and pencil to sketch out a plan as I stumbled upstairs. I'd be busy for weeks now. When I was researching and writing a new paper I rarely spoke to anyone at all. But all during the holidays, whenever Humdinger passed the crèche he apparently removed the second baby Jesus. I guess he was serious when he said one was quite enough. I would replace it. I ordered quite a few. It made me unaccountably happy to know there was always a replacement Jesus at the ready. And finding one missing confirmed for me what I already suspected, that human nature being what it was, someone was always stealing the baby Jesus. Can't blame them for wanting their own baby Jesus, though. Probably they're all keeping them in their bathrooms in their soap dishes. Thank goodness we can afford for everyone to have his own. But that Humdinger is a strange fellow. I've seen him take three or four already. Greedy. Nobody really needs *four* baby Jesuses, do they? Oh well, must let the butlers have their quirks. Strange fellows. Strange profession to get into. Hope he likes his ties.

MELINE

IT WAS JUST TWO WEEKS before Christmas when Uncle Marten, Jocelyn, and I finally made it in to dinner all together again. I was feeling well enough to come downstairs to eat for the first time. My temperature was down now and I was eating meals again with regularity. The puppy, I noticed, followed Humdinger wherever he went, having given up on me because I was always asleep when he investigated my room, or Jocelyn, who slept by day and scavenged by night and, since that first night out, refused to take the puppy with her for fear of losing it. She had found a second aileron and part of a fuselage and was very busy. Mrs. Mendelbaum had an odd glazed look in her eye when we saw her at all, which wasn't very often. I'm not sure she had even seen the puppy yet. But Humdinger provided the puppy with regular meals and let it out and in again. He was the only one who seemed to hear its high-pitched cries and could interpret them. He housetrained the puppy and cleaned up after it. He knew when the puppy was hungry or thirsty, when it needed to go out or have a door opened for it. And finally, because no one else seemed to have thought of it, he named it.

"Aileron!" we heard him calling as we ate dinner. At first I thought he had spotted Jocelyn carrying one and then realized she was with me at the table. Then I thought maybe she'd carelessly left one in view of the house. When I realized that Aileron was what he had named the puppy it opened up a whole other sinister can of worms.

"He knows," I whispered in Jocelyn's ear, casually strolling to her place at the table.

Humdinger was in the kitchen making Mrs. Mendelbaum's tray and putting the finishing touches on dessert. We were having profiteroles. His baking was coming along a treat. I noticed he used a lot of the cookbooks in the kitchen. "Aileron!" he called again. "Supper!"

I looked sharply at Jocelyn to see if she had heard. She had, and her usually ashen skin went just a pale more ashen. Jocelyn and I heard the puppy bounding in and we stared at each other. Our great fear was that some grownup was going to discover what we planned to do and put a stop to it. When Humdinger came in with our profiteroles Uncle Marten said to him, "You named the puppy Aileron, I hear?"

"It's an airplane part," said Humdinger.

"I know what it is," snapped Uncle Marten, which was so unusually severe for him that we all stared. He cleared his throat and furrowed his brow, saying, "Yes, well, I'll be taking my coffee and cake upstairs, do me the favor of putting it on a tray and bringing it to me there." It was also unlike him to order anyone, even the servants, around. He did it so seldom we never even thought of Humdinger or Mrs. Mendelbaum as servants, they were more like weird relatives who had happened in and stayed. And were expected to do all the work. Humdinger quietly filled a proper tray with doily and silver, napkin, cream and sugar, coffeepot, coffee cup, and a silver-covered plate of profiteroles. I hoped Uncle Marten appreciated all the trouble Humdinger was taking, when implicitly ordered to snap to and behave like a butler, which if you'd asked me, Humdinger had been doing pretty well anyhow, not to mention being cook, housekeeper, and nurse.

When they had left the room completely I turned to Jocelyn and said, "He knows."

"Who do you mean, Humdinger or Uncle Marten?" asked Jocelyn, eating, I was amazed to see, her sixth profiterole. Well, had everyone gone mad since I'd gotten ill?

"Humdinger. But what was with Uncle Marten? What's going on? Has anyone *said* anything to you?"

"Only Uncle Marten. He said that he saw me going out at night and I should be careful of the bull. That Humdinger seemed under the impression there was a bull about. Then he asked me what I wanted for Christmas and I couldn't think of anything, so I said a soldering iron."

"Oh, excellent. Couldn't have done better myself."

"Yes, well," said Jocelyn, trying to look her usual irritable self but clearly pleased at the praise. "I couldn't think of all the bits and pieces we undoubtedly need, all the tools. But I thought I'd tell you so you could prepare your Christmas list with the things we need."

"I think the first thing we need is the dolly."

"Yes, I should have told him I wanted a dolly," said Jocelyn, her face falling and looking depressed again.

"But the important thing right now is asking ourselves why Humdinger named the puppy Aileron? Come on, that's not a word just anyone knows. He must know we've found one and have put it in the barn. He must have heard us talking. It's not surprising, the way he pads around like that cat of his, making no noise at all, sneaking up on you."

"If he wanted to ask what we were doing with all those airplane parts, why didn't he just ask?"

"Because he knows what we're doing with them and he wants us to know he knows."

"How could he know?"

"I don't know, but he's strange. Offering you mints like that."

"I like the mints."

"Hmmm," I said disapprovingly because I couldn't for the life of me think why he shouldn't offer her mints or why she shouldn't like them. But there was something going on. Why wasn't he offering me mints? Maybe she was in on it with him. But in on what?

"Anyhow, Jocelyn, don't tell Uncle Marten or Humdinger *anything*. Although I don't think Uncle Marten secretly knows about our airplane parts because can you imagine Uncle Marten keeping *anything* a secret? There's still a lot about both of them that we don't know."

"Well, clearly, and vice versa. Not to mention Mrs. Mendelbaum. Did I tell you I found her once on the way to the bathroom humming and kind of sashaying, like she was dancing with a partner?"

"That must have been a sight."

"Well, it was. I don't know. It's all so confusing. It's all been so confusing while you were sick."

"It isn't any more confusing than it has been up until now, you just didn't have me to sort things out for you." It was strangely comforting to think that I had this role, but Jocelyn didn't think so, she looked at me as if I were crazy, and went upstairs to bed, and I was left again with the grim understanding that I had no role in anyone's life anymore.

The week before Christmas, Jocelyn began to cough. It wasn't much of a cough. In fact, she sounded a lot like the puppy when he was begging for attention. At meals he had taken to staying in the kitchen but making gentle noises that were a cross between a whine and a growl and ended up sounding as if he were clearing his throat in a not terribly effective manner.

"Oh, for God's sake," Uncle Marten would roar.

"Would someone please feed that mutt? HUM-DINGER!"

"He's been fed," said Humdinger, slipping into the room with a pair of covered vegetable bowls. He always made at least three vegetables for every meal in the mistaken belief we would eat them.

"Well then, why is he making that noise?"

"All dogs do that. They want to be fed all the time."

"Presumably not when they're not hungry, though," said Uncle Marten. "My research has shown that the dog, as well as most mammals brought up in the wild, does not acquire neurotic relationships with food the way you or I do."

"Very good," said Humdinger.

"My relationship with food isn't neurotic," I said. "Although I had a friend in school once, Marianne, who ate everything in sight. And another one who wouldn't eat at all."

"Not at all?" asked Uncle Marten.

"Nothing."

"Impossible. She would be dead."

"She was. Eventually. She got thinner and thinner and then she was dead. And then I suppose she got thinner still."

"Rubbish."

"No, she did."

"You must have been very sad."

"Not so much. I didn't know her very well. She wasn't

even a friend really, just someone I ran into in the halls. It was more of a shock. But her parents were very sad. And her friends. I went to the memorial service. Well, a lot of us did. Even the ones who didn't know her that well. And a lot of people cried. Of course, it's easier to cry at funerals. I cried, too. Not because I knew her so well or was so sad but just because everyone else was."

"That's mean," said Jocelyn.

I didn't know if it was mean. I didn't want to think I was mean, but sometimes I saw myself through Jocelyn's eyes and all my good intentions were as dust and I vowed not to speak honestly about anything again.

Everyone was quiet at the table after that and I thought they were all being awkward and silly, thinking I'd put my foot in it because I was remembering death as it was before it had happened to us, but now it would mean something different and I had dredged it up and embarrassed myself. But when I looked around the table to confirm this, I realized I was being paranoid. Uncle had simply stopped paying attention and had stuck his nose back in his book and was taking notes, and Jocelyn, who clearly didn't think about anything I ever said for more than two seconds, was on to the next and demanded that I recite to her the parts of a car. This, as you can imagine, caught me somewhat by surprise.

"You said your father made you learn all the parts of machines you used. So, I guess you're telling me that because you were going to get your driver's license next year, he spent the last year teaching you how to put together a car."

Springing this on me out of the blue was very crafty. I wouldn't have time to look up the answer. If I didn't know it she could assume I didn't know how to build an airplane either. As much as I admired her guile, it infuriated me that even this joint project couldn't be based on trust. I pulled my chair up to hers and whispered, "I can't believe you're asking me to prove what I can do after you spent all those nights out in the rain. Why did you bother to look for airplane parts in the rain if you never believed me? Am I going to have to do this every week from now on? Am I going to have to prove and reprove things to you? Do you trust no one? Do you have faith in nothing?"

"So?"

I sighed. "Well, let's see, there's the carburetor and the cylinder block, head and valve train assembly, oil pump, piston, connecting rods, pins and rings, gaskets and seals, flat lifters, intake manifold, rocker arms—"

"All right," said Jocelyn. "I just didn't want to find out I was spending my nights in the rain dragging airplane parts back to a barn for nothing."

This time I didn't say anything but left the table and went to bed. After all, I might be getting better but I had still been very sick.

JOCELYN

MY COUGH was growing more persistent until I had to admit to myself that despite my superior fortitude, which in some superstitious corner of my mind made me feel I should be able to avoid the viruses that Canadians and Americans succumbed to, I was indeed going to come down with the flu just like Meline and Mrs. Mendelbaum. I was finding it harder and harder to wake up in the middle of the night and chillier and chillier when I did go out, and I didn't seem to be able to warm up when I got back into the house until one day when I was dragging into Meline's room to tell her about the slanted piece of metal I had found, and Meline made me draw her a picture and saw that I'd found a slat, instead of straightening up again from where I'd been bent over pad and paper, I collapsed on Meline's bed. It was so warm and soft. No wonder she had been spending so much time there. I suddenly had the idea that perhaps I'd just stay there awhile and rest.

Meline didn't move from where she sat on the bed studying the picture I had drawn but said matter-of-factly, "Jocelyn, you have a fever. I noticed it first thing when you came into the room. Your eyes were too bright. Your cheeks were too flushed and you looked hot."

"How do you look hot?" I asked. I felt dreamy and warm and not like myself at all. It didn't feel bad exactly, more as if I could be quite content if only I could lie still on a very warm and soft spot with a cool pillow for my face and never have to move again.

"You might as well go to bed," Meline said briskly. "Humdinger will probably end up having to send for the doctor for you, too. Luckily, I seem to be getting better and should be well enough to take your place finding the airplane parts."

I put my head down and it landed on Meline's leg, so she gave me a little shove and I fell off the bed entirely and stayed lying on the floor.

"Oh dear," muttered Meline and started dragging me down the hall to my room, where fortunately Humdinger found us and carried me to bed, where it was discovered I had a temperature of 104. Dr. Houseman came out again and said that I had the flu like Mrs. Mendelbaum and Meline, but unlike Meline hadn't developed pneumonia as a complication. Dr. Houseman and Humdinger seemed to be in the hall talking a lot, but maybe I was mistaken because time had taken on a warp and woof of its own as I lay hotly in the bed. Meline had disappeared completely, but as fuzzy as things were in the fever, other kinds of clarity abounded, and I knew Meline would struggle hardest against sympathy for me, for any of us, when she was most susceptible to it. Sympathy was just a slide into friendship. Avoid all slides. Avoid everything. And I dreamed long sick dreams of playgrounds and swings and teeter-totters and slides I refused to climb up.

MELINE

JOCELYN DIDN'T SEEM AWARE of very much. I'd go peek in on her from time to time to see if she was ready to go out into the rain, but she looked irritatingly hors de combat. She had no real sense of anything anymore, she murmured once when she saw me staring at her, except the sounds of scurrying, like mice. Giant mice. This was mostly Uncle Marten with his Christmas preparations and Humdinger doing Uncle Marten's Christmas bidding. Then there was the normal activity of the household, people coming and going, getting snacks and such, and Mrs. Mendelbaum even sneaked down the hall periodically to look in on Jocelyn. She seemed to have a soft spot for her which she didn't have for me. Probably she had a fellow feeling for her because they were both so stiff and crabby and difficult to be around. She said she wanted to check on Jocelyn because she didn't trust the men. What do men know about illness? Pah! And made Humdinger make endless pots of chicken soup, which she believed cured everything, although Jocelyn wouldn't eat anything except Jell-O and Popsicles when she was awake enough to even do that.

Uncle Marten was apprised by Humdinger that Jocelyn was ill and had asked for Popsicles, so Uncle Marten, in the haphazard way he did everything, kept phoning the grocery stores and ordering boxes and boxes of them, which Sam would dutifully bring over, dropping them, as usual, with drunken abandon anywhere he happened to hover. Some Humdinger and I found, and others melted into the earth and we would find the boxes, a sodden sticky mess of sticks and wrappings, the flavored ice melted.

"It's interesting, isn't it?" I noted to Humdinger once when we went out together to look for them. We had heard the helicopter. "How the thing itself, in the case of a box of melted Popsicles, can disappear, leaving the wrappings so wholly intact. That the Popsicle itself disappears without the wrappings or box being disturbed."

"Like the soul leaving the body," said Humdinger. I think he had a dry sense of humor that he kept under wraps most of the time, the same way he never treated anyone disrespectfully or said anything contrary. I could never live like that myself. That kind of patience went with an ability to keep still and, of course, it was imperative, had been since I got here, to keep moving. You didn't find airplane parts by being patient. You had to have a mission.

Uncle Marten seemed to have his own mission. For weeks he had gone into Christmas overdrive. He was like an elf in a dressing gown, padding from room to room. He had further accessorized himself with a long silk nightcap, which with the maroon velvet dressing gown and carpet slippers made him look like Scrooge. Although, of course, he was the anti-Scrooge. He had stopped sending Humdinger out for packages and started scrounging the grounds for them himself. I was sitting by the fire, Jocelyn was up in her bedroom, and Mrs. Mendelbaum groaned softly but audibly down the hall from her. I watched as the small hunchbacked figure of my uncle went purposefully back and forth, hanging garlands, opening wet boxes full of candles and fruit and ribbon candy and port and glasses and linens and rugs. "Oooo, lookee, lookee!" he squealed once when unpacking a box of special Christmas dishes with gold rims and little Christmas trees printed on them. Because his steps were sort of shuffling, to keep on the backless carpet slippers, he did indeed look like some kind of strange large scurrying rodent. Occasionally he threw on a wool scarf and overcoat and scuffled outside—he kept a pair of carpet slippers just for the outside and would then come in and throw them off where Humdinger would collect them and put them in the dryer quickly in case Uncle Marten decided to forage out again for more boxes in a few minutes. His comings and goings were spontaneous and impulsive and unpredictable. He was like a toddler with new toys inside and candy strewn outside, unable to stay anywhere long with such temptation everywhere. Some of the things he unpacked he whisked immediately out of my sight as if I cared whether or not I saw my gifts ahead of time. Then one day it was time for the tree.

"My dears," Uncle Marten announced at dinner, raising his glass of port ceremonially and not noticing that it was only me at table, but then "my dears" was less a term of endearment than a verbal accessory that went with his new Victorian-gentleman-of-largesse persona that he had adopted for the holidays.

"My dears, it is time for the tree. I propose we all equip ourselves appropriately with axes and saws and similar equipment necessary to the task, and foray out to the steep rise of the bluff, the wooded one with all those lovely little baby Douglas firs, and cut ourselves a tree. The tree-gathering expedition is a time-honored one in North American families." I was pretty sure this was a direct quote from something he'd read about Christmas somewhere.

"Well," I informed him, slowly cutting my meat into teeny tiny pieces and taking my time with my pronouncement in the off chance it would sink in, "Mrs. Mendelbaum is bedridden and Jocelyn still has a fever and I'm not so pert myself, but I *suppose* I could drag myself up a bluff to cut and haul a tree if it was a very small one."

"Oh, we can't have small. We can't have small at all,"

said Uncle Marten, who had changed from Scrooge into Dr. Seuss. "After all, there's that large dolly you wanted. We must have room underneath for that, mustn't we?"

I'd given Uncle Marten my Christmas list as requested, and if he thought it odd that it consisted entirely of tools, hardware, and a large dolly he hadn't given any indication. Now he seemed to be making jovial allusions to it, but unless he came out and asked me just what I needed all this stuff for, I planned to ignore him.

"Besides, we'll get Humdinger. Humdinger, I'll be bound, can drag anything."

So the next day, muffled and bundled, the three of us set out across the meadow and up the steep hill to the Christmas Tree Bluff. Humdinger and I kept trying to point out smaller, more manageable trees at the foot of the bluff, but Uncle Marten seemed set on the really huge fourteen-foot ones toward the top of the hill, and we couldn't talk him out of it.

"I've got simply boxes of ornaments, you see, they've been arriving all month. Of course, a lot of them, well, most of them, got crushed when they were dropped from the helicopter. You'd think that they'd pack them better, wouldn't you?" When we didn't answer—me because I was breathless already, and Humdinger because he never said anything unless he said something polite and encouraging and agreeable, which must limit even *him* on occasion—Uncle Marten just nattered on. "In this day and age." Again there was no word of encouragement from us.

The ground was muddy and steep, and if most of the ornaments were broken, it really seemed pointless to spend the morning dragging an enormous, hard-to-hold, prickly, sappy monster of a tree all the way back to the house. "I mean with modern technology. Bubble wrap and all." We were silent still, which seemed to disappoint Uncle Marten, who never paid much attention to others himself but obviously found it upsetting when people didn't respond to *him*. "I mean, I know they aren't thinking the boxes will be dropped from helicopters. They don't pack them with *that* in mind. But can that really be much worse than the wear and tear of being shunted in and out of trucks and trains and planes?" Silence. "I think not." Silence. "I think not indeed. Careful you don't trip over the fuselage."

I, who was in a trance slogging ever upward through the mud, woke up a few seconds later, it having finally registered what Uncle Marten had said in the midst of his diatribe, and I stared back down the hill. Sure enough, I saw the corner of a fuselage peeking out from under some fallen trees on the side of the path. Then I caught Humdinger stopped in his tracks as well, staring at me staring at the fuselage, and I gave him an irritated look, running up the hill to catch up with Uncle Marten, who had finally found a tree to his exact specifications and was standing in front of it, his arms held wide as if to hug it.

"Great, let's chop it down and get out of here," I said, going for an ax, but Humdinger took it gently but firmly out of my hands and began to chop himself. He was really being awfully pushy if you asked me.

That evening, after we had cut and dragged the ridiculously large tree back to the house and then been unable to get it in through the doors until Humdinger took them off their hinges and removed them, letting a blast of cold air through the house in the process, and after dinner, through which I had to bear Uncle Marten going on endlessly about Bohemian glass ornaments from the thirties, which it seemed he had decided to start collecting, spending thousands of dollars to have them dropped from the helicopter and broken, when I was safely ensconced in my cranberry chair by the fire with a book and a glass of cranberry juice—all the beverages in the fridge were now red and green; currently we had lime Kool-Aid and cranberry juice going—while Uncle Marten ran around with boxes of things muttering to himself and unpacking ornaments and preparing everything for the tree-trimming party he was putting together with hot chocolate and eggnog and cookies and fruitcake, which nobody wanted after such a large dinner, Humdinger made his way over to my chair and I thought, *finally*, because when Jocelyn had been alone while I was ill, he was always sneaking up behind her offering her mints. Finally, he is offering *me* a mint, and I couldn't wait to tell her, but instead he said, "I've taken the liberty of washing and drying all the wet clothes behind the freezer."

Was I being baited? Was he trying to tell me he knew

what we were up to with the airplane parts? I couldn't think of anything to say to this except thank you, but by that time he was already padding out.

And where's my mint, I thought.

I don't think the tree trimming was quite the festive occasion Uncle Marten had anticipated. Humdinger was washing dishes and taking trays up to the ill. Uncle Marten kept falling off the ladder into the branches, knocking the whole thing over. He got scratched up and covered in sap and he kept trying to keep himself from swearing mid-swear, so that he said things like "Da!" in deference to me, I suppose, although I had hung out with my father and his pilot and mechanic friends enough to be inured to such things and in the end it just annoyed me, the idea that I could be so easily shocked with every-thing else that could go wrong in the world, and finally it irritated me so much, it seemed so oblivious to any of our real situations, that I went up to Jocelyn's room, leaving Humdinger, who had finally joined us, and Uncle Marten with only seventy or eighty ornaments still to hang and roughly fifty or so to break still. There I sat on the edge of Jocelyn's bed and said to her sleeping form, "There's a fuselage, or at least part of a fuselage, on the Christmas Tree Bluff."

Of course, what Humdinger knew or how much was the question. "I don't see how he can know what we have planned. It's not like you'd expect two girls to build an airplane and fly away in it just like that. That would be quite a leap of logic." I had taken a bowl of nuts into Jocelyn's room and was sitting on the edge of her bed cracking and eating them. Jocelyn was in the kind of comalike sleep this flu produced, so she wasn't actually hearing any of this, but I didn't care. In fact, I preferred it. I didn't keep a diary and I found coming in and airing my thoughts to a comatose Jocelyn to be extremely relieving. I found myself wishing that Jocelyn, if she must recover, would continue to fall into regular comalike states. It was talking to someone without the bother of having to listen in turn. "Anyhow, you'd better perk up soon. Christmas is coming and Uncle Marten seems to have high expectations about the whole thing. I think he may have plans to tie you to a chair in an upright position if you can't maintain it by yourself."

JOCELYN

I WAS AWARE that Christmas was coming and I was hoping that they would all let me skip it. I was feeling worse and worse and I didn't like to leave my bed even to use the bathroom. I knew my hair was filthy. It hung in long, loose oily strands, but I didn't have the strength to wash it. I couldn't stand the thought of that moment of cold when you get into a bath or a shower before your body adjusts to the change in temperature. It was bad enough when I did have to get out of bed to use the bathroom, my feet touching the cold, bare floors, the energy it took to put on a bathrobe and pad down the hall. And when I coughed now it felt as if my lungs were going to expire afterward, fold up and be good no more. And really, I thought, that might be the best thing.

One night at three in the morning when I was coughing terribly and trying desperately to keep at bay thoughts of how my mother used to sit with me when I was sick, I thought that now there was no one ever to come care for me, no one who would *really* care in that way if something happened to me. I wondered, if no one cared, could you really care yourself if something happened to you? Would you have the strength to care, would it make sense to care, it was almost as if you needed a second opinion about this. Perhaps, I realized, we take our strength without knowing it as much from the people who love us as we do from any resources of our own, and I knew no one in that house loved me. They might like me all right, although I hadn't really detected any of this either, but there was no love there. I sank my hot head in the cool pillows and decided to expire quietly, when there was a tap at my door.

I startled, sat up rigidly, and stopped breathing. Who could be there? It wouldn't be Meline. Meline never knocked. It was as if my mother had heard my thoughts. Could she come to me like this? I had secretly hoped all these months that she would find a way. That her love was so strong that even death couldn't keep her from me if I needed her. But did ghosts make physical noises? Well, of course, they could. There were poltergeists, after all.

"Oh, come in, come in," I pleaded, croaking hoarsely, all the hope I had left in the world pinched painfully into that invitation, but it wasn't my mother who came through the door and I felt once again I had been cruelly led on by the universe to create this terrible moment of expectation and disappointment. It was Mrs. Mendelbaum.

Mrs. Mendelbaum was hunched over, wearing a black bathrobe. Who buys a black bathrobe? It was funereal, and funereal and bath attire weren't congruent. It seemed wrong and bizarre, especially for someone like Mrs. Mendelbaum, whom you'd expect to find in something pink and fuzzy. It was bad enough to have comfort and hope wrenched from me, but now I had to deal with the wrong and the bizarre. Even the newly familiar was unsure. Not what you really thought. Changing before you had a toehold. I fell weakly back on the pillows and stared unseeingly at the ceiling.

"I hert you!" said Mrs. Mendelbaum. "You were coughing batly."

"I know. I'm sorry," I said, thinking, Oh, leave me alone, leave me alone!

But Mrs. Mendelbaum approached slowly across the floor, her tiny arthritic steps and the black bathrobe making it seem like some strange religious rite. "I brought you some of my meticine."

"Oh," I said. "Thanks, but the doctor said it was just the flu. I'm not taking anything except some Tylenol. For the fever. And aches."

"Yes, I know, maideleh," said Mrs. Mendelbaum. "Oy, these doctors, oy, these men. You've no one to take care of you proper, no? Es iz a shandeh far di kinder. If your mother was here she would give you this meticine. A mother knows. It's for the cough. So you sleep. You can't get better if sleeping you don't do."

"I don't know . . ." I said, stalling. I didn't want to be rude and I felt too deflated to argue, but I couldn't just swallow anything this old woman pushed on me. Who knew what was in it? What it was she believed in. It looked like thick black ink. Meline was right, I had no trust, no faith. But why would I?

"I am taking it myself. Didn't I get better? So the proof you say is in the putting."

"Pudding," I said, distractedly. "You can leave it on the table, if you want. It's very kind."

"No, I give it to you now. A dose now. A dose later in the night if you neet it. But only if you neet it and only at night. I have not much left and it's to make you sleep. I was given six bottles, but I haf neet for it as well. My friend Sophie, she makes it in the shtetl. A Polish meticine."

"Well . . ." I couldn't think. What difference did it

make anyway? At worst, it would kill me, and I'd been thinking about that anyway. Maybe, too, my mother had someone send this strange woman to me. Maybe I was meant to be killed here in the middle of the night by Mrs. Mendelbaum so I could join my mother. So I took a spoonful of the black goo that Mrs. Mendelbaum held out to me, and Mrs. Mendelbaum then wiped the spoon on the back of her bathrobe. In my daze I wondered if that's how the bathrobe had gotten so black. How many times had Mrs. Mendelbaum taken the medicine and wiped the spoon just so? She would have had to drink an awful lot of it.

"Goot, goot. You rest now. You sleep, my little angel. I hat angels of my own once." And the way Mrs. Mendelbaum said it, I began to cry because I knew Mrs. Mendelbaum was not giving the medicine to me, now. She was giving it to her own children. She was giving it to them fruitlessly, as if this loving act could bring her back into time with them. It was her own children she was trying to make well and bring back. Over and over and over.

I sat for a second in bed looking at the wall. Mrs. Mendelbaum had placed the medicine bottle on my night table and left. Then what did I begin to smell? Wet earth. Overheated dense air, full of life, the thick mists of the jungle. I was vaguely aware that this was not just the fever. It was some drugged response to the cough medicine, and I felt both heavily sleepy and sharply awake somewhere else. I heard the brushing of the large, heavy fronds against the window and the clickety clackety clack of the train wheels, like large hooves, trotting over the old tracks. Clickety clack through the jungle, clickety clickety clack. Oh no, I murmured feverishly, because suddenly I knew what was coming next. Then I felt it, my mother's hand on my shoulder, patting it and saying, It won't be long now, Jocelyn dear, and we'll be there. I sighed and leaned into my mother's soft body and smelled the faint whiff of her carnation talc and the faint powdery tang of her deodorant. I settled there and turned my head slightly to gaze out the window at the jungle. Every so often there would be a clearing and I would see a village or a fire, women washing clothes in a river, their feet splayed against the tiny pebbles of the riverbed, their knees apart slightly wider than their feet, their perfect balance, perched over the rocks, and the slap wring slap wring of the clothes, accepting and unhurried in this task. It was the rhythm of their lives while my life and what was to be moved hurriedly on down the tracks.

MELINE

THE NEXT MORNING I came into Jocelyn's bedroom very pleased with myself. "Wake up," I said as Jocelyn stared at me. She had hair matted on her head and some stuck to the corner of her mouth with dried drool and something black and brackish. She really looked as if she'd been fished out of a swamp.

"Whah? I'm sick. Go 'way," said Jocelyn.

"You won't want me to leave when you've heard what I've found," I said.

"Will too, guarantee it, go 'way," said Jocelyn, squeezing her eyes even more tightly closed as if there were a chance this would get rid of me.

"Oh, stop it and WAKE UP!" I barked. "You're not *that* sick. You're not even as sick as I was. The doctor said so."

"Fever," said Jocelyn. "Flu."

"Jocelyn, PAY ATTENTION. I . . . found . . . a . . . COCK . . . PIT!" I figured if she cared about our plan at all, this would excite her.

"Don't care," said Jocelyn. "Don't care. Don't care at all." And this time she put the pillow over her head and held it there and refused to make any kind of response to my fervent pokes, even to defend herself.

"Oh, all right. You're of no use when you're sick, Jocelyn. I'll tell you that much. You're really of no use at all." I crashed downstairs and paced around. Now that I was feeling better I didn't know what to do with myself. If Jocelyn had been well we could have begun piecing plane parts together, but it wasn't something I could do by myself. Or we could drag the cockpit into the barn or at least try to. We might still need the dolly for that. I couldn't believe we had come so far and Jocelyn was just lying feverishly around pretending not to care. The cockpit was such an important discovery. I supposed I could get into it and check out the instrument panel, surely Uncle must have been wrong about the planes being stripped of *all* the instruments. After all, he didn't know planes and the story was hearsay anyway. I was dying to get a good look but afraid that it would roll over and things would be further smashed. I wanted to secure it before I got in. Right now it was wedged at a bad angle between some logs.

I decided finally to make a list of things I could do, which would at least give me the illusion that I was doing something. I was sitting on a chair by the fire when Humdinger passed right behind me. I felt him more than saw him. I certainly didn't hear him. I waited expectantly, but no mint. I suspected it might be because I wasn't waifishly pretty like Jocelyn. It was my observation that the waifishly pretty girls of the world got everything, including sympathy, it seemed, and mints, and that if you were ugly you always had to prove that you didn't have an ugly personality to match and so one must develop charm and an easy pleasant interest in others, but I had decided a long time ago that this was too much trouble to go through with every idiot that came along.

I awoke to another gray day and got out my list of things to do. I forgot it was Christmas morning until I heard the bells. Because we had no churches on the island

I put on my robe and searched the house. They seemed to be coming from Uncle Marten's room. His door was open a couple of inches, so I gave it a push. It was some program he had put on his computer, ringing in Christmas morning.

"Good morning, good morning, good morning!" he called to me jovially, scampering down the hall in his Christmas carpet slippers with holly embroidered on them. I sighed and rolled my eyes. The day's festivities had undoubtedly begun. It was going to be a long one.

"You heard the bells, splendid, splendid! Have you tried the Christmas buffet yet? No? Well, it's set up in the dining hall, of course." Apparently, in the short time it had taken the bells of Notre Dame to wake up the whole household our dining room had become a dining hall.

"Bacon, eggs, ham, roast beef, no goose, of course, can't have goose, that's for dinner."

"I don't know, I was kind of looking forward to some breakfast goose," I said.

"Ho, ho, ho, nothing like a little Christmas humor," said Uncle Marten forgivingly. "Now, I must go finish stuffing stockings. Want everyone to have stockings round the fire. Round the fire. Awake the dogs and cats, there's plenty for them, too."

I had visions of rounding everyone up, puppy and cat, who lived their independent lives and were rarely seen, and nailing them to the floor around the fireplace. The morning events were going to be full of interest. I was just thankful I was well enough to withstand all this; it would be awful to have to appear in a weakened state.

I crept downstairs. Then, as I was sitting alone in the semidark "dining hall" with my plate of bacon and eggs, calmly watching dust motes dancing in the one stream of light coming from a window while the rain poured heavily as usual on the roof, down came Uncle Marten dressed to the nines and I realized that I was not going to be able to slop around in my pajamas in his Christmas scenario. He said nothing but had already provided a green velvet dress which yesterday Humdinger had placed on my bed. I trudged back upstairs. It fit more or less because it seemed to be some sort of medieval design, coming nearly floor-length and having a yard-wide waist.

When I came back down and Uncle Marten saw me, he asked, "Where is everyone else? Where is everyone else? This is Christmas after all!" Humdinger was standing with Uncle Marten before the fire, both of them sipping something hot from silver cups. His Christmas outfit from Uncle Marten was a tuxedo but still with the strange butler collar he had arrived with. Humdinger was as composed as always, and Uncle Marten quivering with excitement.

"Right," said Humdinger, and he and I went to rouse Jocelyn and Mrs. Mendelbaum, who was very confused.

"This is not my holiday, bal toyreh! Loz mich tzu ru. I am a Jew!" she kept protesting to no avail. I don't know what Humdinger did to convince her to come down, but she appeared looking shrunken in what I guess was the fanciest dress she had, a kind of awful-looking thing with large orange flowers. Uncle Marten eyed it with consternation. I could see he was thinking that not getting her a Christmas dress as well had been a great oversight. She clashed with all the cranberry and green. But there was always next year! Jocelyn still had a fever of 102, and so Humdinger carried her downstairs still in her pajamas and wrapped in a blanket.

"No dress? No Christmas finery?" asked Uncle Marten.

"No," said Humdinger firmly.

"Are you sure?" asked Uncle Marten, looking at Jocelyn's feverish cheeks and then sighing resignedly. "All right, then. It's a pity. It was a very nice red velvet. But never mind. Maybe that would be more suited to Meline, after all. I think really, yes I do, that the red was the nicer of the two. Meline, maybe you'd like the red dress."

"I don't think a dress meant for me would fit her," said Jocelyn, proving she could still be judgmental even at death's door.

"If it's like my dress it would fit anyone, it's like a tablecloth with sleeves," I said, sitting down with a plop on one of what were now the five chairs before the fire. Uncle Marten apparently couldn't stop buying wing chairs and Humdinger must have brought them in quite recently; they were still damp from being dropped outside.

"And the pets!" said Uncle Marten, clapping his hands together and then rubbing them. "Where are those two, what're their names?"

"Aileron and Kitty," said Humdinger, who was the only one of us who knew. Even I didn't know what the cat was called.

"Kitty? Hmm, not what I would have named a cat," said Uncle Marten. "I suppose you wouldn't think of renaming her? Something from Shakespeare maybe? Let's all take turns thinking of a good Shakespearean name. All cats should have names from Shakespeare if they must have names at all, and if you think of it, why name a cat? They don't come when you call them. Still, if you must, why not Portia? Your turn," he said, turning to me.

"Juliet," I said.

Then he turned to Jocelyn and she followed my lead. "Romeo."

"But the cat's a girl cat, dear," said Uncle Marten, who usually didn't bother us with terms of endearment, but this was Christmas, after all.

"The Nurse, then," she said feverishly and then shivered as if for effect.

"The Nurse?" several of us asked.

"Wasn't there a nurse in that play? I'm sorry, but it's the only play I know and will everyone please leave me alone?" She turned it into one long sentence without pause and we all averted our eyes accordingly. Talk about strange.

"Well then, you, Mrs. Mendelbaum."

"Who would know by Shakespeare? Me ken brechen, I'm not naming your farkuckt cat," said Mrs. Mendelbaum and ate a shortbread. We none of us tried talking to her again. Still, it was obvious that Uncle Marten didn't want to leave her out of Christmas or any naming ceremonies that might come along.

"Well then. Humdinger?" said Uncle Marten.

"Kitty," said Humdinger and thus ended the game.

Good for you, I thought.

"Well, perhaps we had best get on to stockings. Yes, stockings. Humdinger, give me a hand, will you, old boy?" Humdinger followed Uncle Marten into the third-floor bathroom, where, Uncle Marten later told us with glee, he had hidden the filled stockings in the laundry hamper. They carried them in one by one and presented them ceremoniously to us. I could see that Uncle Marten was quite proud of himself. He even had one for himself that he had made Humdinger stuff for him. He had taught him the use of the computer and Internet, which, it surprised me to learn, Humdinger had never used before, and Humdinger had ordered various items he thought Uncle Marten might like. Uncle Marten had paid for them, of course.

"A garlic peeler, very thoughtful, sir," said Humdinger, taking things out of his stocking. None of us knew the protocol here. Were we all supposed to unstuff our stockings one by one, exclaiming over each other's items, or was it to be some kind of free-for-all? As we sat self-consciously fiddling with the items on top and looking at each other out of the corners of our eyes, so as not to appear either too eager or too reluctant, Uncle Marten solved our social dilemma by ripping through his at a tremendous rate, not commenting on anything but sort of tossing items out into a big pile while he exclaimed "ummmm" and "ah" noncommittally and then cried, "All right, then! Let's get on to the games!" Then he noticed that we had not opened our stockings yet and impatiently signaled by a rolling motion of his right hand that we had best get at it, time was wasting.

I went through my stocking and it was full of an amazing assortment of inappropriate things as if Uncle Marten had ordered things willy-nilly out of a variety of catalogs with no attention whatsoever to whom he was giving them to. Mrs. Mendelbaum got a hair curler, a cocktail shaker, and seven murder mysteries, for some reason, and, I could not help but feel, a rather useless supply of bubble gum.

Jocelyn, who less opened hers than let it tip so that things simply fell out to a pile by her feet where she could ignore them in peace, got, from what I could see, a toy truck, several packages of candy cigarettes, and an embosser the actual seal of which I couldn't read but seemed to be for the Zingle Company. Should she ever be in need of papers marked with the Zingle logo, she was all set. Humdinger's seemed to be entirely full of neckties and that handy garlic press, of course. Mine had a flute, an assortment of small rubber balls, the purpose for which was unclear, some packing labels, and some boxes of tea. I offered Mrs. Mendelbaum the tea and Uncle shrieked at me, "No TRADING!" Mrs. Mendelbaum said she didn't want the tea anyway and gathered her things, which I was pretty sure she had no use for, into a tight little pile in her lap and held on to them possessively while glaring at all of us as if daring us to take them away.

"What kind of games?" I asked suspiciously.

"Christmas games," said Uncle Marten, clapping his hands again. The hand clapping at first seemed to be a particularly obnoxious Christmas tic, but then I noticed that it was turning on and off the tree lights. He had some kind of clapper device installed for this purpose and he couldn't seem to stop playing with it all day.

So Humdinger dutifully passed out paper and pens and we were forced to do word scrambles and mazes and word searches and any number of puzzles for prizes that were made up of each other's stocking stuffers. When someone won, Uncle Marten simply swooped in and took something off someone's pile of loot and awarded it to the winner. The first time he tried to take something away from Mrs. Mendelbaum, she grabbed it back and gave him such a look he did not try that again. When we exhausted all his paper games, he started moving our chairs around and announced we were going to play musical chairs, which was when Humdinger declared luncheon served.

"Oh no, not right now, surely it can wait," said Uncle Marten, but "The flan is temperamental" was all the satisfaction he got from Humdinger, who, I noted, was clearing breakfast things and setting a lunch table as fast as his little tuxedoed legs could carry him. It was only ten o'clock, but nobody mentioned this. We all sat at the table, even Humdinger and Mrs. Mendelbaum. Jocelyn, with her steely discipline, managed to stay upright all through the Christmas lunch, which consisted, as per Uncle Marten's menu, of a celery root salad and some flan and a green Jell-O mold in the shape of a wreath with cinnamon Red Hots and Cool Whip decorating the top.

"Women's magazines online are such a source of incredible foodstuffs," said Uncle Marten cheerily. "Have some celery root?" He passed it to Jocelyn, who shivered uncontrollably.

There was a silence as we looked at the ten o'clock victuals on our plates; all of us, I thought, except Mrs. Mendelbaum, must be thinking of Christmases past.

"Light lunch," said Uncle Marten, reading his book on the life of Einstein—one of the stocking stuffers Humdinger had thoughtfully chosen for him—throughout lunch and barely looking up. After lunch Jocelyn begged to go up for a nap and Humdinger reminded Uncle Marten that she was ill, as was Mrs. Mendelbaum, and perhaps we should take a break in the festivities so everyone could admire the contents of their stockings anew in the comfort of their own rooms.

"Excellent. Excellent suggestion and unquestionably in the spirit of the day," said Uncle Marten and, sweeping his goodies together, was the first to retire upstairs. We all gave a collective audible sigh of relief and I thought Jocelyn was going to faint, but when Humdinger came to help her, she just crabbily waved him away, which turned into more of a push from where I was standing, and headed off upstairs, her pile of stocking stuffers still untouched and unexamined on the floor by the fire. Humdinger collected them and later put them in her room and I heard her say something crankily to him before he crept back out again. It wasn't like her to be rude to grownups, but these days she always had the querulous air of someone who had been prematurely roused from a deep sleep.

Uncle Marten rang a little bell at three in the afternoon. We all tried our best to ignore it, but he followed it up by shouting, "It's time for PRESENTS!" Oh, God, give me strength, I thought, imagining what we had suffered with the stockings multiplied. Then I remembered that we had actually given him a Christmas list, so if he had followed it, and I saw no reason why he wouldn't, the tools and things I would need to make the airplane were there and perhaps I could even get started working on it tonight. This excited me so that I flew downstairs.

"Ah, a little enthusiasm at the thought of presents, excellent, excellent!" said Uncle Marten, rubbing his hands together. Humdinger was already there. We waited a bit. Uncle Marten rang his bell a few times again and then, finally, we had to repeat the actions of the morning, with Humdinger going up after Mrs. Mendelbaum. I went to get Jocelyn, who, although she'd had a nap, was still cranky.

"I don't *want* to go down. I don't *want* to have Christmas with a bunch of strangers," she said.

She was only saying what we were all feeling, but it annoyed me to hear it aloud. What good did it do to say it? "Get downstairs. The sooner you open your packages, the sooner I can start building the plane," I reminded her.

"Oh, for heaven's sake," she said, but allowed herself to be led sulkily back down to the wing chair reserved for her. She sat there with her arms crossed over her chest, glaring at the fire. Mrs. Mendelbaum, I think, had had a little private drink of some sort and was looking a bit loopy and stoned. She kept swaying as if she heard music. Uncle Marten sat in a chair and Humdinger fetched us each one present. The opening of them took the rest of the afternoon. Mrs. Mendelbaum, for some reason, was given a large mounted singing fish, which she said confirmed her worst suspicions about goyishe holidays. Uncle said he got it from an overstocks catalog. "Tahkeh a metsieh," said Mrs. Mendelbaum, but as usual none of us knew what she was talking about. I got all my tools, and we were down to the last present when Humdinger put a long rectangular box on my lap. I couldn't imagine what I had asked for that was shaped this way, and I wondered if Uncle Marten had gone out on a limb and gotten me something he'd chosen himself because he thought I'd like it, but this seemed unlikely. He had no idea who I was or what I'd like. Yet he seemed particularly excited by this last present.

"Open it, open it, best for last," he said excitedly, getting off his chair and dancing around me. I struggled with the ribbon. He had wrapped the presents himself and had obviously had Boy Scout training. The knots had taken us forever to undo. "And I must say, Meline, I was ever so happy *someone* thought to ask for one because next to a large toy truck I can't think what Christmas would be without one."

"One what?" I asked ripping off the paper. I sat there flabbergasted. Inside was a large doll that looked a bit like me with its round apple cheeks and blunt hair with bangs. I couldn't think what to say. I hadn't played with dolls in years. Mind you, it was no stranger than getting the embosser that said Zingle Company.

Uncle Marten awaited my response breathlessly, then when I could think of nothing appropriate to say, blurted out, "It's your dolly! The dolly you requested."

I tried to smile, but it was more just a matter of stretching my closed lips across my face. I looked up at Uncle Marten and saw Humdinger eyeing me, a tiny glint of amusement that he was unable to conceal peeking uncharacteristically out.

"Thank you," I said finally.

"Now for dinner!" said Uncle Marten, clapping his hands in excitement and inadvertently turning on and off the tree several times. It was disco Christmas. We sat in the chairs while Uncle Marten handed round eggnog, rumless for me and Jocelyn and with rum for Mrs. Mendelbaum, who if you asked me didn't need anything else to make the day merry and bright, she was merry and bright enough when she came down, but I was too depressed to discreetly point it out to Uncle, who hadn't noticed anyone's state anyway. The light was fading, which should have made the house feel cozy and even more Christmaslike with the millions of candles Humdinger had lit about the halls, but instead it felt like a large, empty death. Sorrow lay around our feet, like warm water, coming six inches up our legs. We waded through it. Everything was damp and wet, not shiveringly cold, but you couldn't wade from room to room without being aware of it. Always there. Not life-threatening, just lapping against your legs so you could never move freely in the way you had before. I told this to Jocelyn, who, as usual, was very literal and said, "Six inches of water can be life-threatening. There was a woman in my mother's guild who drowned in a creek during a drought. There wasn't more than six inches of water there. Probably less."

"How is that possible, Jocelyn?" I argued. "It wouldn't

cover her head, so unless she was facedown, it wouldn't go in her nose, and even if it did, all she would have to do is turn her head."

"She couldn't turn her head, my mother said. She took a terrible fall and she didn't have the energy for it."

Well, it sounded very bogus to me, but I didn't feel like arguing at that point. It seemed to me that if you drowned in six inches of water you just weren't showing much spunk. I went to sit next to Mrs. Mendelbaum by the fire. She kept taking sips from a small flask in her pocket. Whatever she was drinking didn't look like liquor. It left a thick black rim around her lips.

"Can't wait for goose, eh?" said Uncle Marten delightedly on his way through the dining room. Fortunately, he didn't wait for an answer. He turned the stereo on—one of his presents from himself to himself was a whole stereo system, which he had spent an hour hooking up while the rest of us sat glumly. Finally he herded us all to the dining room to the haunting sound of some boys' choir singing carols in a big echoey cavernous church. The music ringing in all that empty space only accentuated our own dilemma. I think all of us would have given anything to just go to bed at that point. Even Uncle Marten, though clearly loopy on eggnog, seemed to be fading.

"Well then, well then," he said when we were all seated. "I suppose now is the time to carve the goose. *Wait*, the crackers! The Christmas crackers!" Then we all had to pull on the end of these strange party favors that made explosive sounds that clearly freaked out Mrs. Mendelbaum. Inside each was a toy, a hat, and a joke or witty saying. We had to read these and put on our hats. Fortunately, no one was called upon to exclaim about yet another useless toy. Then Uncle Marten grabbed his large dangerous-looking carving paraphernalia again, and holding a carving knife and fork in his hands with his paper crown on his head, bid Humdinger to bring in the goose. The goose was duly gotten and Uncle Marten hacked at it, looking all the while at an illustration from a book he had bought on goose carving. I kept thinking of the geese which we saw flying over the island in October in beautiful long-necked V's and which still hung around, swimming in the ocean and pecking worms out of the meadow, and I wanted to throw up. I knew for certain that although I'd come a long way from my vegetarian ways I could not eat goose. The only one who ate it with any gusto was Humdinger, who had also cooked it. Mrs. Mendelbaum picked at hers, but she was clearly by now stoned out of her mind and kept asking people to pass her the side dishes, which she would then look at as if she'd already forgotten what she'd wanted them for, before passing them on untouched. This kept everyone busy and her too busy to do much eating. Jocelyn put food dutifully on her plate but just took sips from her ice water and finally fell asleep in her chair, something I was reasonably sure she had never done before in her life. It was quite some time before anyone else noticed it. Uncle

Marten took one bite and stopped eating. "So this is goose?" he said as if he didn't quite want to believe it. "Well, it's simply horrible. No wonder most people eat turkey. No wonder there's not a run on geese at Christmas. Because who in their right mind would want to eat them. I, myself, can't go through with it. It's very fat, isn't it? It's . . . fat." I think it was the breaking point for him. Up until then he'd been able to ignore the fact that no one else was full of Yuletide spirits, that living in the house together did not make us one big happy Christmas family, that the cat wasn't going to wear her Christmas collar or the dog his Christmas sweater. The stockings sucked, the presents sucked, and the goose tasted disgusting. I think it was finally occurring to him that you could buy all the props you needed for Christmas but people were not props. Humdinger looked at Uncle's face and then noticed Jocelyn and carried her off to bed. Mrs. Mendelbaum asked where dessert was, and while Uncle looked vaguely around for the Christmas pudding, Mrs. Mendelbaum started passing side dishes again. That's when I left the table.

I went upstairs. How I spent the rest of the evening was nobody's business. I didn't even have the energy to go look for airplane parts. I lay down on my bed trying to decide whether to go to sleep for the night even though it was only six o'clock when there was a knock on my door. I couldn't imagine who it could be. Nobody ever came to my room, not since Jocelyn had been too ill to move, but it wasn't Jocelyn anyway, it was Humdinger with a mint.

By the New Year, Jocelyn's fever went away. Dr. Houseman, who had come in periodically to check on us when her schedule allowed, didn't need to come anymore, but Uncle's radio phone rang a lot and it was usually her and she usually wanted to speak to Humdinger. "What do you talk to her about?" I asked him at breakfast, but Uncle called down for him before he had a chance to answer me. I struck up small conversations occasionally now because otherwise I would talk to no one. Uncle, as if demoralized by the Christmas fiasco and his miscalculations of what would be enjoyable for all of us, hid his nose in a book during dinner and often didn't come down at all, sending me his apologies through Humdinger and requesting a tray. When he did come down, I tried to talk to him about something I thought might interest him.

"So," I said, "I read somewhere that someone predicted the end of the world in 2010."

"People are always predicting the end of the world, Meline," said Uncle Marten without looking up from his book.

"But they have it all charted. Don't you think that the world would end slowly, not, as they predict, in one big quick bang, so I mean it wouldn't really end over a year but over a period of years, wouldn't it?"

"The world is not going to end, Meline. It's been around for billions and billions of years. Mankind is a mere blip in its existence. Man might end, but there will be other life-forms. Most likely cockroaches."

"Cockroaches live a long time, don't they?"

"It's not that cockroaches live a long time; it's that they've been around for billions of years before man and will probably be around billions of years after. If anything survives, it will probably be the cockroaches. We'll all probably come back as cockroaches in our next lives. Learn to scuttle."

Mrs. Mendelbaum didn't seem to be recovering from her bout with flu and stayed in her room. I could hear her busy stockinged feet waltzing now and then. It was a sad, macabre sound. The cat had never been good company for anyone but Uncle. The puppy followed Humdinger about or went tearing around the island on his own, coming back for dinner or naps by the fire. Humdinger, as I said, had a lot of conversations with Dr. Houseman. So I was on my own. It was okay, I guess. I read quite a bit; there were a lot of books certainly; and I searched for airplane parts and finally admitted to Uncle the kind of dolly I wanted. I went up to his room. It was a conversation I did not want Humdinger to overhear. Uncle was sitting hunched over his desk.

"You see," I began after he had waved me wordlessly into the sanctum. "I meant a dolly like the kind used to transport things. A small flatbed on wheels."

"I see, I see," he said briskly with none of his usual opinions and spirit. It was obvious that he was still embarrassed about Christmas and didn't wish to impose on any of us again. "Well, then see that Humdinger gets one for you. He knows how to use the Internet now and I've hooked him up downstairs, so there should be no problem."

"I'd rather he didn't know about it," I said.

"Why?" asked Uncle Marten, pulling his half glasses down to his nose tip and looking at me sharply.

"I'd just rather he didn't. He . . . prowls," I said.

"I see. One of your games, no doubt. Well, never mind. I'll order it for you, only please don't bother me any more right now. I'm most busy with hydrochloric acid and titanium."

"Thanks," I said and backed out. I felt curiously deflated. Here I'd been avoiding Uncle Marten, and when I finally went to see him I found he wanted to avoid me even more. And I wanted to tell him that I knew he had tried his best at Christmas. It wasn't his fault it had been such a disaster. It was no one's fault. How could it have been otherwise when we all missed our old lives and knew so little really about each other. But to tell him any of this would be the first step to connecting to someone since my parents' death. Even this feeling of compassion, wanting him to feel better, was treacherous. It was a slippery slope to forming a bond and I couldn't start that again. So I said nothing.

The dolly was dropped the following week. I knew Uncle was always as good as his word, so after he said he'd order it, I kept a sharp eye and ear out for Sam and every time I heard the helicopter I raced out to find his drop before Humdinger could. I picked up a lot of late-arriving Christmas things and groceries until the dolly was finally dropped in a huge crate. I had a time uncrating it, but after that it was easy to wheel to the barn. The next night I maneuvered the cockpit out of the tree with only slight breakage on one end, onto the dolly, and into the barn, and then I went to visit Jocelyn.

"Well, I did it," I said, sitting on the edge of her bed. She was staring glassy-eyed at a magazine and seemed to have no interest in what I had or hadn't done.

"The dolly. I got a real one and uncrated and moved it and got the cockpit and moved *that* into the barn. But it wasn't easy, Jocelyn. You know I'm not a whiner, but your fever is gone and you're really going to have to concentrate on getting better and getting out of bed because I'm going to need help soon. I can't fit pieces together alone. Someone, for instance, has to hold up ends while I solder and bolt things together. Ideally, we'd have a whole crew but we need at least two."

"Why don't you ask Humdinger?" asked Jocelyn in the queer little spaced-out voice she always used now.

"Why don't I ask HUMDINGER?" I roared. "What is the matter with you anyway?" I spied the almost empty bottle of black cough syrup on her bedside table. It had been full the week before. I picked it up and said, "How much of this stuff are you drinking these days?"

"None," she said, sitting up suddenly and snatching it out of my hands.

"Jocelyn, you're hardly coughing anymore. Should you even be drinking this stuff? What has Dr. Houseman said about it?"

"She says it's good for me, take lots," said Jocelyn, putting the bottle back on the table but keeping one hand resting close to it.

"You haven't told her you're taking it, have you? Where did you get it? Did Humdinger give it to you?" And suddenly I saw him as an evil figure. Lurking in his big shoes and Frankenstein-monster body. A giver of strange potions. Perhaps the mints were poisoned. A snoop.

"No, the doctor did," said Jocelyn, her hand snaking slowly back toward the bottle.

"The doctor prescribed it? Or did Humdinger just tell you the doctor prescribed it?"

Jocelyn looked at me blankly as if she couldn't decipher such a difficult question.

"Oh, for God's sake, are you even sick anymore or are you just stoned? Tell Humdinger you can't take this medicine. He's trying to poison us, Jocelyn, and he knows about the airplane building. He snoops."

"Didn't get it from Humdinger," said Jocelyn in a tiny, listless voice, putting her magazine down on her stomach, closing her eyes, and not too subtly dismissing me.

"Well, I don't suppose you'd tell me if you did," I said. "Listen, you've got to pull it together and help me build the plane now. Or have you lost interest in that, too?"

"Tired," said Jocelyn, and that was all I could get her to say, so I left her, to work on the plane. I had given myself a schedule. A schedule and a lot of airplane chores. I found keeping exactly to the schedule worked best. I made notes to myself. I tried not to deviate from it by a minute. When I did I kept track of it in a notebook I labeled, "Deviated Minutes." Busy, I muttered to myself, busy.

I began to work at night in the barn with the big flashlights set up that I had asked Uncle to get me for Christmas. It was quiet and peaceful in the barn. I wasn't afraid of the bats anymore or the dark or things getting me. The only thing I occasionally thought about was the bull. No one but Humdinger had seen it, and I was inclined to think he was mistaken, but there was hay in the hayloft and that seemed to give some credence to its existence. On the other hand, Uncle had mentioned that the barn and some of the outbuildings had been here when he bought the island. That people had a farm here long before the Corps used it. Perhaps they had bulls and some of them had escaped and become feral. How long did bulls live?

Putting together the airplane was concentrated work and it absorbed me completely, trying to fit things together, being careful with the tools and the soldering. Trying to imagine which piece I would find next and how it would fit in place. More and more I was beginning to realize that I would not be building an exact replica of a plane but rather a kind of flying machine. But that's all we needed. Something that could get aloft.

JOCELYN

I SAT BY MY BED. I had heard Meline go out. It was safe now. I had only a bit of cough medicine left in the bottle. I didn't know if it would be enough for tonight. I doubted it. I seemed to need more and more to get to the place where I fell first into a lovely, relaxed state of oblivion, past caring, where my body felt good, where I wondered why I had ever felt so wretched anyway. Everything was fine. Everything was as it should be. I wanted to go tell everyone about it, but truthfully there was no one to tell. Then I'd be sleepy, terribly, heavily sleepy and lie down, thankfully falling into a deep, drugged sleep, and then I'd be on the train again. On the train with my mother. Riding, riding, and everything was fine most nights. Sometimes I got to the part where there was a jolt and screaming and light, but usually I awoke before this and, even when I dreamed it, often forgot this part upon waking, so it didn't matter. I took the last little bit of the cough medicine. But I wasn't feeling euphoric. I felt only mildly relaxed and I was afraid it would wear off before I fell asleep. It was the middle of the night. I couldn't wake Mrs. Mendelbaum up to ask for more, could I? I really didn't want to bother her, but she wouldn't care if I just slipped in if her door happened to be unlocked. As long as I didn't wake her.

I went into the hall, grabbing the wall for support now and again. I'd been sick, so of course I was wobbly. The floor was cold on my bare feet, but I didn't want to disturb anyone with slipper sounds. Shoe sounds. Noisy. Maybe Mrs. Mendelbaum's door was unlocked. Well, probably there weren't locks on any of the bedroom doors. If there had been one on mine, I would have locked out Meline. But if I'd locked out Meline, Mrs. Mendelbaum wouldn't have come in with the medicine. I'd never have had the medicine. No. She knocked. I would have let her in. It would all have worked out. Whew. Why wouldn't you put locks on bedroom doors? It made people use desks in front of them. Why *would* Uncle have put locks on when he planned to live alone? Yes, but if he planned to live alone, why so many doors? Probably he was prescient. That's probably what he was. Oh, the universe was a vastly mysterious thing and Uncle was the most mysterious thing in it. I laughed. I found I was much funnier after I took the medicine. No, I was always as funny as I wanted to be, but I wanted to be more when I took the medicine. No, I appreciated my humor more. Was always funny. Very humorous sort, really. That was the problem with most people. They didn't appreciate themselves enough. They certainly didn't appreciate *me* enough. Meline didn't. What was the deal with Meline? She didn't get me at all. I would tell her this when the medicine wore off. Which it was going to do soon if I didn't hurry.

I put my finger to my lips. A little reminder. Shh, shh, as I turn door handle. My mother never said "Shh." She said "Hush." Hush hush. Uh-oh, that makes me want to cry. Hush hush. That's what she would say to me probably most nights now if she saw me in such a state. Why do I say "Shh" if she said "Hush?" Shouldn't I have picked up "hush?" Why choose "shh?" Difference between people who were shhers or hushers? Oh well, hardly matters.

The door creaked open. Mrs. Mendelbaum was dead. Gasp. No, not dead, just lying on bed with all her clothes on. Still, better make sure. Don't want to be accused of stealing from dead person. No, but live person stealing perfectly okay. Ha ha. Told you was funny. Drag self over to bed to check. Yep. Still breathing. Not dead. Only resting. Mrs. Mendelbaum snorted and I jumped. Stop that, silly snorting woman. All right, where is darned cough medicine? "Okay, medicine, where are you?" Then I cover my mouth. What do I think am doing, talking out loud? Going to wake poor dead Mrs. Mendelbaum. Shh shh, must differentiate thinking thoughts from saying thoughts. Not to mention dead person from resting person. No thoughts out loud. Be quiet. So exhausting having to control mind like errant pet. Who called a dog Aileron? Stupid name for a dog. Stupider name for an airplane part. No one picked good names anymore. What kind of name was Meline? Cruel Meline, that's what she was. No mercy. No feeling. She must be Canadian. Ha ha. No, American. Well, she wasn't British, that was for sure. Not like us. Mummy called us Brits at heart. No doubt. Try dresser drawer. I have hidden things in underwear drawer when little. Chocolate bars. Bad for teeth. Maybe medicine there. Nope. Just underwear. Ugh. Horrible underwear. Must wear ugly underwear when get old? Why bother getting old? Only thing to look forward to, ugly underwear. No. Choose better underwear, is all. Where else? Closet. Ugly shoes here, too. Why so much ugliness in world? Not enough cough medicine, that was why. Oh no, falling asleep. Can't do that here. Big scandal. Must find bed.

Creep back down hall, but forget to close door to ole Mendelhoffer's room, but my room close, so no matter. Wow. Surprised such big wallop from such small dose of medicine. Must keep that in mind. Thought had to take more. Maybe just impatient. Don't be impatient. Haven't enough to last. Have none left actually. Have to get more. Maybe stop looking airplane parts, start looking for shtetl. Don't know what shtetl is. Serious impediment. Don't tell Meline. Thinks she knows everything. Oh well, tomorrow is other day. Is that Humdinger closing Mrs. Mendelbaum's door? Strange, Humdinger. Think is nice but what's with mints? Little mint obsession, ask me. Anyone tell him chocolate bad for teeth? Or *Uncle?* All that chocolate. Still have some left. What's with men and chocolate? Like it so much, maybe should marry it. Ha ha. Joke. Weak joke. Feeling weak. Well, at least Humdinger doesn't see me. Swing into room and bang door closed. Accident. But big noise. Whoops. Oh well. Got mice. Probably think mice did it. If think at all. Nobody in house thinks. That's problem. Canadians again. Seem to be everywhere. Fall on bed. Feels so nice to fall, going down, down, down. Effortless. No longer have to work so hard. Just let go. Nice. Oh, there it is, click clacking of train. Oh, Mother. Oh, Mother, here she comes, here she comes. All okay now.

I got up the next morning and had tea and toast. Quite a bit of it. I was getting my appetite back. Probably all these good sleeps I was having. Then I thought of the empty cough medicine bottle. Something would have to be done about that today if I wanted to keep having these good sleeps. If I couldn't find Mrs. Mendelbaum's cough syrup stash myself I'd just have to tell her that I needed another bottle. And she'd just have to give it to me. She started this. If she wouldn't give it to me, I'd threaten to tell Uncle. I don't think he'd be too thrilled with her passing out medicine without asking anyone. But would she care if he knew? It wasn't much of a threat if she didn't care.

Just as I was thinking all this she came into the room without knocking.

"Jocelyn, maideleh, I need to borrow back the cough syrup. I have run out."

"You've run out!" I barked, pulling myself up. I had been slumped on my pillows, balancing a teacup on my stomach.

"You are better now and what do I have left, nothing. Shmek tabik. I know, I know how it is for you, as it is for me. Es vet gornit helfen. Nothing will help. The others do not understand. You and I know, it is over, our little time, our little pyesseh. And I have no energy to start new. And I think you, too, have no such energy. But ich hob es in drerd, enough, give me the medicine."

"I can't," I said in alarm. What did she mean, she had run out? I thought she had bottles of it.

"You won't, you mean, but it is enough for you. It is my cough syrup. I have lent it to you for just the short time. To get over the hump."

"You don't understand," I said, falling back on the pillows wearily. Now what would we do? "I ran out, too. Last night. I took my last dose."

"Show me," said Mrs. Mendelbaum in steely tones, and I took the empty bottle from where I kept it under my bed and handed it to Mrs. Mendelbaum. There was nothing but the smeared remnants on the inside of the bottle.

Mrs. Mendelbaum took my water pitcher and slowly dribbled some water into the bottle, shook it up until a filmy gray liquid evolved from the water and the few drops of tarry medicine clinging to the sides of the bottle, and quickly drank it.

"Now it is finished," Mrs. Mendelbaum said and left the room.

I felt strange all afternoon. I was doing nothing these days in the afternoon but waiting until it was time for the cough medicine. I hadn't even realized that this was what I was doing, that it lent a whole rosy glow to the afternoons, the anticipation. The mornings were getting over the haze I awoke with from the medicine, the afternoons were the happy anticipation of the medicine. The evenings were bliss and then sleep. Sleep like no other. I had found a way to live. It was impossible that this was taken from me. I was furious and irritated and in a panic. And it was worse now that I felt better. When I was feverish I hardly needed the medicine because I could fall into deep sick sleeps and lie in semicomatose states when awake by myself. But now I was conscious and had energy and I didn't want it. I wanted the haziness. I wanted the sleep. I wanted the blissful oblivion.

I guessed Mrs. Mendelbaum was feeling the same way because I heard shouting from her room. Humdinger had brought Mrs. Mendelbaum her supper tray and Mrs. Mendelbaum was screaming, "Take it away! Can you nothing well do? This by you is food? Go, go and leave a

poor old lady to sleep. Maybe I will drop dead in my
sleep! Or better, maybe you will!" I knew how she felt.
Others were unbearable. Their noise. I had gone out in
the hall to listen and Humdinger came out of Mrs.
Mendelbaum's room before I had a chance to scuttle back
into mine. For a second he eyed me there and then he
looked at Mrs. Mendelbaum's door and a thoughtful look
came over his face. I slipped back into my room and
closed the door, breathing hard. I mustn't panic. And I
mustn't yell like Mrs. Mendelbaum. If I yelled like Mrs.
Mendelbaum everyone would know. I mustn't let on that
being without the medicine made any difference to me
at all. On the other hand, what did I care what they
thought, any of them? What did I care about anything?

MELINE

WHEN I WENT OUT THAT NIGHT I was furious with
Jocelyn. Malingering. I had heard my father use this term
about airplane pilots who got drunk and called in sick
and then sometimes stayed sick for a few days. I took my
heavy flashlight and headed off into unknown parts of the
island. There were still bits and pieces of the island not
covered. Unless you walked up and down in straight lines
over every inch, there were lots of copses and hills and
tiny clearings you would miss.

When I had gone out the day before, angry with Jocelyn for not seeming to care anymore about the only important thing we had to do on the island, build the flying machine, I had stormed off across the fields and realized that there was a long peninsula yet unexplored. I headed there tonight. Everything looked different at night and somehow we had circled around the same parts of the island over and over, leaving this peninsula unexplored. I marched toward it, full of angry energy, hoping to find an airplane part that we particularly needed, that would fill her with envy for the moment of discovery. Then with her appetite yet again whetted for our project, I would torture her with indecision: Should I or should I not allow her back in? Had she displayed the proper attitude in all circumstances? I trudged with great stomping feet across the meadow with this on my mind, and I probably would have headed in the direction of the peninsula if it hadn't been for sudden thoughts of the bull. I stepped in something nasty, and for a moment when it occurred to me that it was some kind of animal droppings, I gasped and thought of Humdinger's bull.

"Oh, gross, Aileron!" I said because he had been running around the meadow and was now standing behind me sniffing my shoes. I flashed the light down. Most likely it was from deer, but what if it wasn't? My heart at that second began to beat rapidly. Suppose Humdinger was right, after all. I grabbed Aileron under my arm like a football and started to run.

I didn't know where to go because I couldn't concentrate on holding the flashlight upright and Aileron under my arm and run and panic at the same time. Something had to go. It was enough to remember to hang on to the flashlight, and then it occurred to me that this was making things awfully easy for the bull, so I turned it off and ran in the dark for a while and then, when I didn't hear the bull in pursuit, I tiptoed in the dark for a while, worried that I might actually be moving toward the bull, except that I heard nothing. Not a whisper of bull breath or the sound of hooves thundering across a meadow. Not a sound. So I tiptoed noiselessly on. Aileron cooperated by making no sounds either, which surprised me, you would expect him to protest being suddenly picked up and carried away by someone who up until then had shown him no attention or affection, but apparently he wasn't a grudge-holding type of puppy. Either that or he was just drop-dead stupid. We walked a long way in the dark until I felt confident enough to turn on the flashlight, half expecting to see the bull walking noiselessly behind me. But instead what I saw made me drop the puppy in fright.

It was a gravestone. Not just one but an entire circle of them and Aileron and I had somehow managed to walk between them, like doing a maze in the dark, and we were now standing surrounded by them, in the middle of what looked to be a small private cemetery. Had I kept going in the dark without turning on the flashlight at that point I would never have known they were there. In the very middle of this circle of graves was a pile of broken planes, wings and bodies and cockpits and ailerons, fuselages, elevators, stabilizers, it was all there. The remnants of all the planes that had crashed, everything I would need to build a flying machine, with one plane almost intact in the center. If I moved debris, I could just attach the necessary parts to that one. I read the names on the stones, Second Lieutenant John C. Hooker, Second Lieutenant William Macdonald, Second Lieutenant Daniel Levesque. Someone had buried the Corps of the Bare-Boned Plane, carefully marking their graves, crudely scratching their names in stones, gathering their broken machines. I wouldn't have to drag things to the barn any longer. I could put it together right here.

JOCELYN

I WAS WELL ENOUGH to take a bath for the first time in a while. The water running through my filthy hair felt like heaven, but halfway through rinsing it I began to shake uncontrollably. I'm not ready yet, I thought, and quickly rinsed off, wrapped myself in a towel, and sat on the toilet shivering for a moment before I had the strength to dry off and get back into my nightgown. I padded softly down the hall. It was easy to walk quietly now that I had lost so much weight, I could feel that there was hardly anything between my bones and the air. When I got to my room I stood silently for a moment staring at Mrs. Mendelbaum, who had her back to me and didn't even know I was there until she happened to turn around.

"What are you doing in my room?" I whispered, so surprised to find her there that my voice couldn't be called up from the depths of my throat. I caught a glimpse of myself in the mirror looking like a wraith with my long hair wet and tangled, shivering on the carpet by my bed.

"Where is it? I must have," said Mrs. Mendelbaum, making a fist and advancing threateningly toward me.

"Have what? What do you mean?" I asked, backing toward the door.

"You know. The medicine. The medicine I gift you from the goodness of my heart and which you stole and hid."

"I showed you the empty bottle. I finished it two nights ago," I said, alarmed.

"No, you could not have gone through it so fast. You are too thin. So much would have killed you."

"I did, Mrs. Mendelbaum. It wasn't so much. It was only a half bottle when you gave it to me."

"Gif it back."

"I don't have it. Really. But listen, Mrs. Mendelbaum, we have to get more."

"*We* don't have to do anything. It is *my* medicine. It is mine. Sophie got it for *me*."

"Where did Sophie find it?" I asked, thinking there was no sense dealing with Mrs. Mendelbaum anymore about this. She was clearly crazy. Any medicine that came to the island she would claim as her own. But I could get some if only Mrs. Mendelbaum would tell me where.

"Sophie makes. All the women in her shtetl make it so."

"Well, we have to get more, that's all."

"From Sophie?"

"Yes, of course. I'm sure that Uncle can arrange to have it delivered like everything else."

"He will drop it like everything else, that meshugener pilot, he will break it. Er zol vaksen vi a tsibeleh, mit dem kop in drerd."

"Yes, that's true," I agreed. Sam would be sure to break the bottles. Nothing glass survived Sam's deliveries. "Let me think. Let me think. I know. Sophie must bring it herself. Would she? Would she come on a helicopter and let herself be dropped from a ladder?"

"No, not Sophie never. She does not like planes. But she would come by boat. We must a boat find for her."

"But there aren't any boats, Mrs. Mendelbaum, the ferries don't stop here," I said, climbing into bed now that the danger of an attack from Mrs. Mendelbaum seemed over. I was so tired it felt as if my bones must pulverize right there in the sheets, leaving nothing but a skin bag full of powdered bone.

"Sophie must find one. She must find one and deliver us the medicine. Many bottles."

"Oh yes," I echoed weakly. Many bottles. "Mrs. Mendelbaum, if she knows how to make it, she can make it on the island. She can teach *us* to make it." This was the obvious way. If we learned to make the medicine ourselves we didn't need Sophie anymore. We didn't need anyone.

"I will speak to your uncle and you must speak to him, too. To make him find for Sophie a boat."

"How am I going to ask for a boat for your friend? Why would I ask him this instead of you? It will sound suspicious." I did not want Uncle to suspect a link between me and Mrs. Mendelbaum. I did not want him to find out about the cough medicine.

"That is true. That is true. Yes, you are a bright girl. Well, you must speak on my behalf. That it is your observation that I an old sick woman am, in need of a friend to care for me and keep me company."

"Yes, but would he agree to more people? He doesn't seem to like people."

"Ech, he will agree to anything, that one, if you promise to leave him alone."

"Yes, I suppose he might. So I say you need Sophie. But will she come?"

"She will come," said Mrs. Mendelbaum, falling weakly into a chair as if her legs had suddenly collapsed beneath her. "I can always make Sophie do what I ask. She has no strength. Now go. Find your uncle and beg him to find a boat to bring Sophie."

"I will, after I sleep. I'm so tired," I said. But after Mrs. Mendelbaum left I was not able to sleep. I hadn't been able to sleep properly since I ran out of medicine, and it was beginning to frighten me. Instead I lay exhausted with my eyes closed, hopelessly counting sheep and saying the alphabet and doing everything I knew to lull myself into oblivion, but it wouldn't come. When midnight came I began to worry that I had permanently lost my ability to sleep without cough medicine. Later, I heard Meline come in and come upstairs. I opened my door a crack. I could not stand lying alone in the dark like this anymore.

MELINE

"GOOD, YOU'RE AWAKE," I said when I saw Jocelyn poke her head out the door. "I told you you were getting better. You won't believe what I found."

"An airplane part," said Jocelyn, shivering.

"Are you really that cold?" I asked. I was, after all, soaking wet but I wasn't shivering. Of course, Jocelyn's bones were sticking out now. She had been thin when she came to the island. Now she was skeletal. She looked as if every morsel of food would be visible heading down the digestive tract. "I'm not cold. Why are you always so cold? You'd better start to eat more."

"I can't eat more. The thought of it makes me sick. And I can't sleep," said Jocelyn.

"Well, of course not. You've done nothing but sleep for days on end. You're slept out. Bound to happen sooner or later. Good. Listen, I'm making tremendous progress now with the plane." I was about to tell her how I had taken the tools out of the barn and moved the operation to the cemetery, which I was pretty sure Humdinger hadn't discovered yet. There was everything I needed there for a serviceable flying machine and I was going to be finished with it much earlier than expected. This was pretty exciting, but for some reason all Jocelyn wanted to talk about was Mrs. Mendelbaum and her friend Sophie. I had heard this about invalids: that they become very self-absorbed and blow up the minutiae of life way out of proportion, so I tried to listen patiently even though, clearly, she was bonkers.

"And, Meline, listen, this is very important. *Very* important; Mrs. Mendelbaum wants her friend, Sophie, to come here. She wants Sophie to care for her. She says she can get Sophie to do anything. I am supposed to ask Uncle to arrange a boat to bring her here because Sophie won't take planes. But I'm so tired, Meline, so could you ask Uncle?"

"I don't know. If Sophie comes, then there's less for Humdinger to do. We want to keep Humdinger occupied."

"I'll keep him plenty occupied. I promise. I'm still real sick."

"Oh, you are not."

"I am. I tried to take a bath and I couldn't. I haven't the strength. Humdinger can take care of me instead of Mrs. Mendelbaum. I'll ask him for tea trays constantly."

"What is this weird friendship you have formed with Mrs. Mendelbaum that suddenly her friend coming is so important to you? The two of you are thick as thieves. I'll be surprised if she isn't adopting you." I sat on Jocelyn's bed and thought morosely about this. I could see it. Mrs. Mendelbaum adopting Jocelyn and taking her off the island. The two of them living happily ever after in some light bright modern apartment in Vancouver, engaged in real life, going to rock concerts, out to dinner, Jocelyn going to college on Mrs. Mendelbaum's savings. Sitting down to eat brown meat and savory puddings together. The two of them going to the theater, shopping, restaurants, Sunday walks on the waterfront. Happy as clams. It was because she just lay around looking pathetic, not doing anything. I had done nothing but work. I had kept busy. So, of course, Mrs. Mendelbaum liked Jocelyn better. Of course, she felt sorry for Jocelyn. Jocelyn reeked pathos. Jocelyn said nothing and closed her eyes. It felt as if any tenuous connection we had built on a joint project was swiftly slipping away. I hadn't wanted Jocelyn as an ally especially, but it was humiliating to lose her to Mrs. Mendelbaum.

"Sure," I said defeatedly. "I'll ask Uncle." If nothing else, it would show her that if she picked Mrs. Mendelbaum over me she was losing someone who can be unselfish and magnanimous even against her own best interests. That should make her think twice because I honestly didn't think Mrs. Mendelbaum had exhibited these qualities. And I needed Jocelyn back. I could work pretty well alone with the almost intact plane I had found, but I might still need her for lifting, holding, and steadying. I didn't want to burn bridges completely with her yet.

The next day I went upstairs to see Uncle Marten. I knocked loudly several times and finally went in. He was hunched over his desk, his eyes going back and forth from the computer screen to something he was scratching away at on a piece of paper.

"Excuse me!" I said and then again more loudly, "EXCUSE ME!"

He turned around distractedly and it took him a moment to get me in focus. Whatever he'd been working on was clearly still running through his head and he was reluctant to leave it.

"Can I interrupt?" I asked.

"You already have," he said irritably. "As you see, you already have." Then he sat there looking at me with his lips pursed and his brows furrowed, not saying anything, waiting for me to go on.

"Well, the thing is that Mrs. Mendelbaum is sick, as

you know, and Jocelyn is, too, but Mrs. Mendelbaum would like her friend Sophie to come and care for her."

"Care for her what?"

"To take care of her."

"Why? Isn't that what that Humdinger is doing or supposed to be doing? Didn't I hire him for that?"

"No. You hired him to be the butler. Now he's doing his job and Mrs. Mendelbaum's and caring for Jocelyn and Mrs. Mendelbaum, and I guess Mrs. Mendelbaum just wanted a friend here. You know, in case she got worse. She has no family left. Sophie is her only friend."

"Well, just how sick is she?" asked Uncle Marten. "Is she in danger of expiring soon?"

"Well, not soon," I said, stalling. I didn't want to leave any false impressions that would worry him. "More like soonish. Soonish rather than laterish because she is, after all, older. I mean *much* older."

"Is she really so very old?"

"Don't you remember Jocelyn said so?"

"Do you think she dyes her hair?"

"I guess so," I said.

"Because it's awfully black."

"She must dye it, I suppose. I mean, I've never seen her dye it."

"She'd have to get hair dye, then. Wait a second, I've seen her carrying around bottles of something black. That's it! She says it's cough medicine, but you can bet on it, that's the hair dye."

"Hair dye? Jocelyn has been drinking it."

"Jocelyn has been drinking hair dye?"

"She says it's cough medicine, too," I said.

"Well, that which doesn't kill us makes us stronger. Are you sure?"

"*She* says she has been drinking cough medicine that Dr. Houseman gave her."

"Oh well, then I suspect she has. What's that got to do with Mrs. Mendelbaum's black hair dye? Really, let's try and stay on topic for two seconds. Oh, say, I don't think I've ever seen any roots either," said Uncle Marten.

"That's a good point. If it were dyed, you'd expect to see some roots occasionally. When she's flying around, you do see a lot of gray underneath."

"Yes. But then, if she doesn't dye her hair, what is she doing walking around carrying bottles of black hair dye?"

"White roots, if she's really old, her hair would be white, wouldn't it? Not just black with gray underneath," I said.

"Yes. I haven't seen a single white root. But perhaps she keeps them covered in that hair dye and that's why she walks around with it. Maybe she is always doing, what is it that women call it? Touch-ups! Or maybe she's not so old."

"I think she is."

"She doesn't look it."

"But I think she is. Anyhow she *seems* pretty old, doesn't she?"

"In what way?"

"I don't know. Set in her ways. Like she's lived her whole life already. Like there's no place to go. Like she's just kind of resting now on her time left before, you know."

"Before she dies."

"And she talks about Nazis. If she was young in Nazi Germany, she'd be very old by now."

"I'm going to call Houseman to come in and get a look at her." He picked up his radio phone.

"Oh, I don't know if that's such a good idea. I don't think she'd like that."

"Why ever not? She's sick, isn't she?"

"Yeah, but I think she just wants this friend."

"Oh, for heaven's sakes, we can't possibly have anyone else living here. The house is bursting at the seams already. I really think I must take a stand."

"Yes, but think how you'll feel if Mrs. Mendelbaum were to die alone."

"Die? Who is talking about dying? Besides, no one in this house could die alone if he wanted to. We're crammed in here like sardines."

"I'm sure it's only for a short visit, anyway."

"All right. But let us make that clear at the outset. People do so often seem to show up on your doorstep and then stay forever." Then, when he realized what he'd said and to whom, Uncle Marten blushed a deep red and looked frantically confused, immediately launching into a new train of thought, hoping, no doubt, I hadn't noticed, but I had and my stomach sank slightly. I had not known our presence bothered him so much. I hadn't cared about being wanted. I had wanted to be left alone. But I hated to think of myself as an annoyance. An annoyance he could do nothing to rid himself of. I was glad for the change of subject as well.

"How can you talk about people dying like that?" he asked. "It's very bad for the digestive system to even think of such things. I'm sure she isn't dying at all. I'm getting Houseman anyway because you can't have people just dying unnecessarily all over the house. Of course, people are going to die and sometimes at *your* house, but not just cavalierly because you've *left* them. Because you've forgotten to have the doctor in to check. Even though I'm certain it is completely unnecessary. But there it is, you've put the thought in my mind yourself. You've only yourself to blame." Uncle Marten pressed a button and got the hospital and left a message.

"I'm surprised that you know her number. I'm surprised you remember her name," I said. He never remembered things like this.

"How can I forget her? She calls about fifteen times a day. Not to speak to me, oh no, it's Humdinger she's got her eye on. He won't last long. No backbone. She'll have him married and bundled over to Vancouver before the summer, you mark my words. There'll be a summer wedding with everyone in long floaty white dresses and flowers and barefoot. Probably want to do it here on the island. Come to think of it, probably would want to raise their children in this very house if she could get a job here, which thank God she cannot. Everyone wants to come here. I just don't understand. I just don't understand."

"There's another thing . . ."

"Well, there always is these days, isn't there?"

"Mrs. Mendelbaum wants you to arrange a boat to take Sophie over here because she is afraid of planes. She won't take the helicopter with Sam."

"But Sam doesn't drive a boat," said Uncle Marten, going back to work. "He never has. He doesn't like the ocean. He likes the air. Can't think why."

"But he can't be the only person who could get a boat here."

"Hmmm? No, probably not. The laws of probability say otherwise. Anyhow, I'm busy. Have Humdinger attend to it. Isn't that what he's here for?"

"I think you hired him to answer doors."

"In point of fact, Mrs. Mendelbaum hired him, and as I recall it was so he would worry—but worrying doesn't seem to be his strong suit, so let's see how he is with boat procuring. Now leave me alone. No more things. Go away."

It was always easier and harder than you thought it would be with Uncle Marten, but you could never predict which would be the easier things and which the harder. I sighed and went downstairs to give Jocelyn the news. She was pacing and scratching and didn't seem interested particularly. So then I knocked on Mrs. Mendelbaum's door and she was lying on her bed moaning.

"Mrs. Mendelbaum . . ." I said.

"Go away."

"I've got good news."

"Oh, oh, oh," she said and put a pillow over her head.

"Mrs. Mendelbaum, do you hear me?"

"Oh."

I heard her muffled groans.

"You can call your friend Sophie and ask her to come here. Uncle Marten says it's okay. He says Humdinger can arrange a boat for her."

"Oy," moaned Mrs. Mendelbaum. She seemed to like to vary her distressful exclamatory syllables. Then she started snoring just like that. For a second I was afraid it might be a death rattle, so I ripped the pillow off her face, but it was furrowed and she breathed heavily in the deepest, most miserable-looking sleep I had ever seen. It looked as if instead of giving her relief sleep was torturing her. "Mrs. Mendelbaum?" I said, but she continued to snore and I decided not to wake her. Jocelyn could do the rest. She'd probably rather have the news from Jocelyn anyway.

Maybe Uncle was right and Dr. Houseman *had* better see Mrs. Mendelbaum. I left when it was clear that she was going to hear nothing I said, and went back to Jocelyn's room. She hadn't stopped scratching or pacing and I wondered if maybe she had measles on top of everything else. She was still far away. Almost as far as Mrs. Mendelbaum appeared to be. They were a pair, all right.

"Listen, Jocelyn," I said, "you're going to have to tell Mrs. Mendelbaum about Sophie yourself because she won't listen to me."

Jocelyn just nodded as if she had no time to speak to me. As if I was interrupting her pacing.

No thank you from anyone. No acknowledgment. I left and went to my room. When I got there I realized that I hadn't even told her about finding the plane cemetery. I started to go back and stopped. What was the point? It was clear that she no longer cared.

Day after day passed alike. I slept or sat alone. My nights I spent working in the cemetery. Then one day I realized that to follow me out to the cemetery without being spotted was beyond even Humdinger's sneakiness. It was easy to see me going into the barn from a window in the house and even easy to sneak up to the barn and spy on me. But the cemetery was a long way from the house. And, besides, I thought, who cared anyhow? What could Humdinger do about it—the plane was almost built. If he hadn't done anything to stop me up until now, it was doubtful he would in the future.

There was a deep quiet in the house now. Jocelyn and Mrs. Mendelbaum never left their rooms and Uncle never seemed to notice. He was preparing for a conference and ate silently, reading through dinner. The puppy remained with Humdinger and the cat with Uncle Marten. In such deadly silent aloneness, my thoughts began to stray too often to home. Some nights I didn't even care about going out to the cemetery to work and would roll over to go back to sleep. This frightened me more than anything. I could not afford to lose momentum.

The day Sophie arrived I was the first one to see her. I was on my way to the plane cemetery when the boat landed. It was a small fishing boat and I thought Humdinger was very resourceful and wondered how he had procured it. The captain or fisherwoman or whatever you called her helped Sophie out and into a dinghy, which she rowed to shore, and then the woman pulled the dinghy with Sophie in it up onto the pebbly beach so she could get out without getting her feet wet. I stood and watched and almost ran over to escort her to the house, but then I decided no, I was not a welcoming committee, my plane was coming along a treat, and I would be departing soon. I did not wish to raise her hopes that she had a friend in me, so I shrugged to myself as I watched them scan the island for the house, and walked on toward the cemetery, where I spent a long day reattaching one wing where it had separated from the fuselage.

When I got in for dinner that night, Sophie was sitting at the table. Humdinger had set a place for her where Jocelyn used to sit, mid-table, but she had pulled her chair and place setting cozily next to Uncle Marten and was engaging him in conversation, which seemed to bemuse him, but politeness dictated he stop working and pay attention.

"Ah," he said as I sat down. "Here is Meline. Meline dear, this is Miss Babilinska. You must keep her entertained. You really *must*." He emphasized this a bit too heartily. Humdinger brought in pumpkin soup, and this seemed to distress Sophie, who kept trying to jump up and take courses from him all through dinner. It was clear she had never been served by a butler before and she seemed to think it was beneath Humdinger's dignity. But from what I had seen over the last few months, Humdinger's dignity was unassailable and had nothing to do with menial labor. In fact, Humdinger's dignity seemed to derive from being able to do menial labor, competently taking care of the things that needed to be done. Humdinger's dignity seemed to derive from the fact that he didn't worry about his dignity. Sophie, in apparent agony, watching Humdinger serve, had a small knot between her eyes even though Humdinger kept trying to reassure her and gesture for her to sit down and stop worrying. This was what he *did*, after all. I dug into my soup enthusiastically. I was chilled to the bone and my hands were red and raw from working with cold wet metal all day.

"I'm sorry I'm late," I said. "I lost track of time." I'd been working with a particularly difficult joint. There was a huge piece of metal missing where the elevator was and I was going to have to rig something. I was still not sure how to cut metal. I would have to go on the Internet and see if I could get some information.

"Tut tut, not at all, my dear. I have been telling Miss Babilinska that in the future I will be unable to eat dinner with the two of you. I have so much to finish before I leave for this conference. Fortunately, with her arrival, the two of you can dine together."

"How is Mrs. Mendelbaum?" I asked Sophie politely because presumably she had spent the afternoon with her. Better her than me.

"Miss Babilinska has informed me that Mrs. Mendelbaum is doing very well. But it is a great comfort for her to know that she has a friend here."

"A bosom companion," said Miss Babilinska, stuffing her mouth with meat. Humdinger had brought in the plates, and after a short wrestle, Sophie had let him do so. I had heard Mrs. Mendelbaum call her Sophie originally and now I was finding it difficult to call her Miss Babilinska, which was a mouthful anyway. There was sliced brisket, and pierogies, which I assume he made especially for Sophie's welcome, and tzimmes, which were candied carrots and mashed potatoes and Brussels sprouts. He didn't bother putting brisket on my plate because by now he knew what I ate and didn't and didn't trouble me by offering me things he knew I wouldn't want. He was as aware of things as Uncle was unaware. Because he was so aware I began to have nervous knots in my stomach; maybe I underestimated him, maybe he could do something to stop me from completing my flying machine. Maybe he was simply waiting until the last second to scuttle my plans. We were so close to flying.

I could hear voices coming from the kitchen.

"Who's in the kitchen with Humdinger?" I asked.

"Ah. That would be the doctor," said Uncle Marten, looking at me meaningly, raising his eyebrows and touching the side of his nose. "She came over to examine Mrs. Mendelbaum, who wouldn't let her in her room, by the way, causing quite a ruckus. Yes, you missed that while you were gone wherever it is you go all day. And then Dr. Houseman went to examine Jocelyn, who wasn't getting well fast enough to satisfy her, so now she has had the brilliant idea that she should move into one of the quickly disappearing free bedrooms where she can keep an eye on both of them."

"I don't understand, doesn't she have to work?" I asked.

"Sam is taking her back and forth now and she is staying here apparently. She has a suitcase with her. I saw her bring it in."

"Well, she can't do that, can she? I mean, it's *your* island, Uncle Marten."

"Well, it *was* . . ." said Uncle Marten, absentmindedly going back to his book.

Humdinger brought dessert in at that point and Sophie ate her ice cream doggedly as if she were afraid someone would take it away if she didn't get it down promptly. So it wasn't until after dinner that she even bothered to look at me, and when she did it was with large, empty eyes. There are some people who you know are simply not too swift by looking at them. I could see why Mrs. Mendelbaum had said she could get Sophie to do anything. She would not be hard to push around because it was clear that she could have no ideas of her own. She had the hanging jowls of a basset hound but also the large trusting sad eyes. But she had no interest in me any more than anyone else in that house, she was there for Mrs. Mendelbaum. And she seemed to be in awe of Humdinger for some strange, basset hound reason of her own.

One evening after dinner when Sophie had left before dessert because Mrs. Mendelbaum had asked her to bring dessert up on a tray for the two of them, Uncle Marten turned to me and said, "How long does she plan to live here?" Sophie was spending more time eating with Mrs. Mendelbaum, so Uncle had apparently forgotten his threat not to come down to dinner and was sneaking down to meals again. We could sometimes hear the sound of their Yiddish drifting down the stairs. It gave the house a strange international flavor, Yiddish upstairs, English downstairs, as if we were the UN.

I shrugged.

"Well, has she moved in?"

I shrugged again.

"Well, let me put it this way, did she have a lot of *stuff* with her when she arrived that she unpacked and put folded neatly into drawers?"

"I really don't know, Uncle Marten," I said, nonchalantly toying with my rice pudding. "I wasn't in when she arrived. I didn't see what she unpacked. She did seem to have a lot of cartons in the dinghy. But I can't say for certain those were hers because I didn't see them taken out. I left before they unloaded them, if they did. They might have belonged to the boat owner."

"The boat owner?"

"Yes."

"Why would the boat owner have a lot of cartons in a dinghy?"

"Well . . ."

"That's it. Trust me, that's the tip-off. Cartons. She has moved in. I have lost another bedroom."

I shrugged again. I was becoming a great shrugger.

Sophie was keeping Mrs. Mendelbaum occupied. I had hoped that with her arrival, Mrs. Mendelbaum would sever ties with Jocelyn and Jocelyn would rejoin the air-plane building, but I was beginning to accept that Jocelyn didn't ever want to get out of bed. It no longer felt like a joint project. I was working feverishly. I left the house early in the morning and worked in the rain until I was drenched, coming in at lunchtime to change clothes and eat and go out again until dark. It was staying light longer and longer and I was vaguely aware that trees were budding, but I didn't care. Humdinger seemed to find my wet clothes no matter where I hid them and they ended up washed and dried and folded neatly on my bed. This seemed pushy to me. As if he were emphasizing that I could have no secrets from him, but even this didn't bother me particularly. It didn't seem to matter if he knew anymore as long as he didn't stop me. Rainy day followed rainy day. It didn't warm up gradually like spring did at home. Instead daffodils bloomed, blossoms came out on trees, but the rain remained a gray driving constant and every day was like the one before.

I was sitting in a wing chair in front of the fire one evening, eyeing Humdinger carrying a basket of my laundry up to my room, when Dr. Houseman, who had just come dripping into the house, having arrived by helicopter, plopped beside me. She shivered and ran her hands over her rain-drenched face and then held her wet hands before the fire.

"Whew," she said. "Long day. Thank goodness Sam was on time. I think I would have slept at the hospital or at home tonight if he hadn't been. I didn't have the energy to wait around on that windy helicopter pad. It's beastly out there."

"Why don't you ever sleep at home?" I asked. "Why bother to sleep here? Jocelyn and Mrs. Mendelbaum aren't that sick, are they?"

"Well . . ." She looked as if she were about to tell me something and then stopped. She sat quietly for a moment in her chair. She was one of those people comfortable with her own silences. Then she said, "They're something of a mystery to me, I must admit. They aren't getting better as fast as I would like. I can't tell if it's some kind of secondary infection or depression. And, of course, Humdinger asked me to keep an eye on things. Medically."

Oh, Humdinger did, did he? So the romantic feelings were not on Dr. Houseman's side alone. "If you ask me, Jocelyn is just stoned. She keeps taking this cough medicine and who knows where she's getting it. You're not giving it to her, I bet, but Jocelyn says you are. And I wouldn't be surprised if Mrs. Mendelbaum is taking it, too, because at Christmas she was going around with this flask of black stuff that looks a lot like the stuff Jocelyn was taking. And I can guess who is giving it to them if you're not."

"I'm not giving them any medicine, no. So who do you think is giving them cough medicine?

"Humdinger!" I said. The cat was now certainly out of the bag. But if someone was poisoned it was as well that I made my suspicions known ahead of time. And she should know what she was romantically dallying with, if you asked me.

To my surprise Dr. Houseman, instead of seeming shocked or concerned, allowed a thin weary smile to cross her face. Then she just sat there for a second with it frozen as if having her own little joke.

"I'm sorry," she said, finally coming back to. "Oh my, it's been a long day. Why would Humdinger be giving Jocelyn and Mrs. Mendelbaum cough medicine?"

"He's trying to poison them. I'm telling you, the man, well, he has suspicious behavior."

"No doubt," said Dr. Houseman and smiled again. "Listen," she began, leaning forward and putting a hand on my forearm, but just then Humdinger came in and offered to get Dr. Houseman dinner and she followed him into the kitchen, winking at me as she left.

Well, of course she wouldn't listen to you, you ninny, I said to myself. What did I expect, if Uncle was right and she was making a play for him? She wasn't going to think he was a poisoner. Worst of all, now she was probably going to tell him that I was onto him, and it would be twice as hard to catch him. On the other hand, perhaps, so alerted, he would cease drugging Jocelyn and Mrs. Mendelbaum long enough for Jocelyn to recover sufficiently for me to take her to the plane. The aircraft was almost complete. I had only a bit of bolting left and it would be done. Maybe two days' work. Would Jocelyn be well enough in two days? If I could get her as far as the dolly, I could wheel her there. I wasn't sure that she would care about going anymore, but it seemed the right thing to do. As if I must think for her now that she could no longer think straight herself, and keep my promise to take her with me. I tried to imagine what Humdinger would do about this. Would he come racing across the meadow after us? I had never seen him race before. But how else could he thwart us? Would he somehow slip the medicine into me as well? Into my food? I was so close to being done with the plane that I vowed not to eat again. Then there would be no danger of becoming permanently stoned like Jocelyn. On the other hand, what did Jocelyn need the plane for if she had the cough medicine? She'd found her own way to fly above it all. She'd found her own way out. At that moment, I cut her loose. I don't know why I ever thought she and I had to do this together anyway. I had done it all mostly alone and I could complete it alone.

The next day I finished bolting the machine. I turned the engine over and I should have been frantic with joy to hear the miracle of this sound, this engine I had brought to life after so many years idle and useless, but instead I sat in the pilot's seat, worn out and feeling flat. I looked out the rain-streaked windshield to the blossoming trees and felt nothing. None of it really mattered. Without Jocelyn, there was no one who would even see me leave. It felt odd to have no witness, not even one you didn't particularly care for, in your life. I tried to rouse some emotion in myself. Perhaps I just needed to eat something. Maybe I was at such a low energyless ebb because I needed food. I hoped it was something I could fix so easily because I could no longer reason myself out of this sense that none of it mattered or ever had. I dragged myself back through the rain to forage something uncontaminated in the kitchen, and on the way I almost tripped on a box that was lying sodden in a furrow. Another of Sam's drops, one that had been sitting in the rain for a very long time so that the cardboard had soaked through and all but disintegrated, leaving the contents spilled in the mud. I pawed through it and carried it back to my room.

What I spread on my bedroom floor were the muddy remains of our photo album, pictures of my mother and father. I had taken none with me. This must have been sent some time ago by the executor of my parents' estate. I had not seen my mother's or my father's face in months. I did not want to move or see or feel or think. I lay on my bed facedown all day and hadn't the energy to raise my head or bring my face out of the pillow. I no longer wanted liftoff or even flying above it. I wanted nothing. I remembered those bodies in the doorways in East Vancouver. How little I had understood them then. How little I had known how much worse things could get.

When twilight came I trudged for the last time across the meadow and through the woods to the plane. I started the engine and moved the throttle. The propeller was spinning and I moved forward down the rutted remnants of the runway, jolted now and then so hard that my head hit the ceiling. Then things began to go inexplicably wrong. The plane tilted when it shouldn't have and a wing hit the ground. I lost control of the wheel and the engine made strange noises. I was thrown sideways and tried desperately to attain an upright position, through crashing noises. The plane began to spin in circles. I looked for the instrument panel and remembered there was none. I grabbed frantically at the wheel and tried to move the throttle back, but it was stuck, and I was growing dizzy watching the line of trees in the distance go around and around. Then something hit the back of my head and that was all I knew.

When I awoke the back of my head was bleeding. It was dark out and I was chilled to the bone and a little nauseous. For a minute I thought I had flown and crashed; then I looked out the window and saw the lights of the house in the distance and the stand of trees where the cemetery stood and knew that the plane had fallen apart before it had taken off. I put a hand to where my hair was plastered with blood, and groaned, and then pulled myself out of the plane wreckage. All along the ground were fallen plane parts as if the plane had simply fallen apart piece by piece as it taxied to liftoff. But how was that possible? I'd checked it all myself. Humdinger! The thought so filled me with fury that although I was feeling dizzy and nauseous, I felt a burst of angry adrenaline that flooded my legs with sudden strength, enough to see me back to the house. I stormed up to the bathroom, shed my filthy clothes on the floor and cleaned my cut, ran a bath and sat there in fury until some warmth returned to my limbs. Then I put on clean clothes and went to Uncle's study, not sure what I was going to demand, that Humdinger be fired perhaps. How dare he?

How dare he interfere? He had gone too far this time. I pushed Uncle's door open slowly, but he was asleep at his desk. I was about to wake him up when I saw, heaped on a corner of his desk, holding down some paper, a pile of airplane bolts.

I was so startled by being completely wrong in my assumptions that I crept out without saying anything at all. Uncle, not Humdinger, Uncle had seen me working on the plane. Uncle had removed the bolts. Uncle had *known* what I might do. How? It was too many questions. I went to bed. I would build another plane! But when I awoke in the morning I knew I was done building planes. I saw Jocelyn heading for the bathroom, looking groggy as usual. She was going to crash her plane in a slower, surer way, but Uncle didn't seem to see this. I went out and walked to the meadow to check the plane and confirm my suspicions. Sure enough, all the bolts I had spent so long putting in had been equally carefully removed. I followed the trail of plane parts back to the cemetery and there, in the space underneath where the plane had always stood, I saw for the first time the three gravestones lying flush with the ground: Second Lieutenant Vincent Knockers, Second Lieutenant Michael Knockers, Second Lieutenant Gary Knockers. I sat down on the grass and thought for a very long time.

Later, when I could bear it, I went up to Uncle Marten's room. I didn't know quite how to introduce the topic of his and my father's deceit. And Jocelyn's father's, too, I guess. They had all lied to us. Or at least had not told the whole story. I opened his door all the way from the six-inch gap he always left for the cat. He was sitting at his desk with his back to me, scribbling away as usual. I cleared my throat twice and finally he turned around.

"Oh, Meline!" he said in surprise.

"I went out today to where the plane I built stood. Or what's left of it. I was looking to see if it had fallen apart because the bolts were removed," I said, looking down. He said nothing. When I looked up he was just nodding his head. Not denying or admitting it but not offering any kind of explanation or apology either.

"Well, where the plane used to be, there were three gravestones flush with the earth."

"Second Lieutenant Vincent Knockers. Second Lieutenant Michael Knockers. Second Lieutenant Gary Knockers."

I nodded.

"There were six of us brothers. Or six and a half actually. I was the pilot that stowed away on the helicopter and turned our father in. It was your grandfather who had the idea of the Corps of the Bare-Boned Plane. It was a good idea, I always thought it was a good idea. It was sacrificing the men to it that was the problem. He took it too far." Uncle Marten looked distant and tired. "Donald and your father were still living at home with our mother. Vince, Gary, Mike, and I were all officers in our father's corps. Anyhow, I saw Vince's plane go down, and after it crashed I thought, we all thought, my father would stop this nonsense. He wanted to make good pilots—why would he allow them to be killed? We thought he might pack up the whole operation. Especially since it had been Vince. Send us all home. But he just kept sending pilots up. We didn't know what to do about it. We were young. We couldn't believe it would continue. I didn't see Gary crash. The other officers told me at dinner. Gary and another member of the corps had gone down together. Mike crashed while I was on the mainland, turning in my father. It wouldn't have been a bad idea if it had *worked*. Learning to fly without instruments. But it didn't. He should have stopped after the first plane crashed and he didn't. He kept going. Well, when I told them what was happening, the bigger brass came over and put an end to it. Our mother lost a husband and three sons. They had to put her in a sanatorium, a kind of a nuthouse. And not a very nice one because we couldn't afford better. I went to visit her there. She'd always been a very sane, practical woman. We'd had a good family life. Good Christmases. Those sorts of things. We thought she'd get out before long, you know, pull it together, but she cut her wrists. She left your father and uncle in foster homes. I went off to college."

I stood on the carpet. I didn't understand. I didn't understand how he could sit there so calmly and tell the story. Or how Uncle Donald and my father could have become pilots after that. How they could teach me and Jocelyn to fly. "I don't know how you went . . . Unbearable, so many of them. Unbearable. I don't know how you went on when it happened," I said.

"Well, it will happen. And if you go on, it will happen again. I don't want you and Jocelyn to leave now. That may surprise you. It surprised me. But I don't. But you will. And probably pretty soon. You'll go on to college and then maybe get married, have families, move away. And then we won't need Humdinger anymore and he'll go. And that lovesick doctor, when he goes, will have no reason to stay around. Not that she was ever invited to move in in the first place, but let's not get into that again. Mrs. Mendelbaum I'm not so sure we ever really had. Sometimes it *is* unbearable," said Uncle Marten.

"I don't want to build another plane. That passed . . ." I began.

"Good," said Uncle, picking up his pen again.

"But how can you be so matter-of-fact?"

"Well, it was a long time ago."

"I don't ever want to feel like that, that it was so long ago that I don't care about my mother anymore or my father. Like getting on a train and leaving my parents waving goodbye. That's what I see every time I think of it. I see myself standing on the back porch of one of those cabooses. You know the kind I mean?"

Uncle Marten nodded.

"And I'm waving and they're waving and getting

smaller and smaller in the distance." I stopped and Uncle Marten said nothing, just looked at me. "I, well, I don't think I can do that. It would break my heart if they thought I could leave them there. I don't think I can ever do that, leave them behind like that. So that means I can't go anywhere either. I'm just whirring up above it all in one spot."

"You should have built a helicopter, not an airplane," said Uncle Marten.

I laughed even though I don't think he was trying to be funny. It was the type of thing that would occur to him.

"Ah well, you see I view it a little differently," said Uncle Marten, putting his pen down again and swiveling his chair slowly back and forth with an abstracted expression. He tented his fingers. "I see it like a lake. And when you have to be parted from someone, for whatever reason, you just leave that part of the lake."

"But they're still in the lake?"

"They *are* the lake. So are you." Then Uncle Marten went back to scribbling.

"How do you know this is true?" I asked.

He swiveled his chair around and looked at me long and hard for a second. "I don't know it's true, Meline. I *hope* so. But sometimes I think we believe these things only because the other is so unthinkable."

Uncle went back to scribbling at his desk and I went down to Jocelyn's room.

I sat on the side of Jocelyn's bed and waited for her slow, drugged awakening. I didn't tell her yet Uncle's story or mine. Instead I said, "Jocelyn, how do you know for sure that they're dead?"

"Wha'?" she asked sleepily, then fell back on the pillow. "Why are you asking this now?"

"Because I am," I said.

"You don't want to know," she said wearily, pulling herself up to a sitting position. "Not really."

I sat silently for a while. I wasn't sure she wasn't right. Then I said, "It was really awful, wasn't it? You saw them, didn't you?"

"At two o'clock the next day it was my turn to go identify the bodies." Jocelyn stopped and began to cry. I put my arms around her. And my plane came slowly down, down, down on ground I hadn't even known was there.

Later I told Jocelyn about the cemetery and the extra uncles. That was when I remembered that Uncle Marten said there were six and a half of them, so I went back to find out who the half was, and it turned out it was Sam.

Sam's mother had been a floozie who had an affair with Uncle Marten's father for a short time while she was on vacation in Canada. While Sam was in Vietnam trying to stay alive to return to her, his mother, with nothing much in her life but her constant worry about Sam, found she got to sleep with a judicious blend of sleeping pills and vodka. One night she found she couldn't sleep even with her usual dosage, so she dosed herself right out of the picture and slept not only till dawn but forever after. Her neighbors, maybe not the world's most upstanding citizens, noticed that she didn't seem to be about anymore, but they only shrugged. Her constant nervous chitchat about her son who was in Vietnam whenever she cornered them in the elevator or by the mailboxes had not made her popular. So they didn't find her until she began to smell, and they became very, very irate as the odor lingered for weeks. They told Sam all this when he got home to California and was trying to piece together what had happened, and so he cut out for Canada to find his biological father and nicer neighbors. It turned out his father had died in prison when he was in Vietnam. It would seem that although Sam had gone off to war with great trepidation, North America was where all the casualties were. When the prison chaplain told Sam his father was dead and that he'd never mentioned having a son named Sam, it precipitated a round of drinking that he never really recovered from. So, having nowhere else to go, but being half-Canadian, he stayed on and got himself fired from six different private helicopter companies before he read a small article in a local paper about Marten Knockers buying the island where the Corps of the Bare-Boned Plane had gone down. He put two and two together and called upon Uncle Marten, who was a little disconcerted to find himself with another brother, but was in need of a way to have things delivered on and off the island and gave Sam the job. Sam would never put down on the island, though. "A little fussy, that," said Uncle Marten.

And then there was Humdinger! Dr. Houseman came to me to ask me more about the cough syrup and when I told her what Jocelyn had told me, that it was homemade stuff, she just shrugged, and said, oh well, these old home remedies, and dismissed it. When I said I bet she was glad that it wasn't Humdinger poisoning everyone, you didn't want to date a poisoner, which was bold but I wanted to see if Uncle was right, she laughed and said that she couldn't date Humdinger even if she wanted to because he was a priest. Sophie's priest, in fact. Impossible, I'd said. Sophie was Jewish. She went to shul with Mrs. Mendelbaum. She spoke Yiddish.

But I was beginning to see that I really hadn't known anything about anyone. Dr. Houseman filled me in on Sophie's story, which Humdinger had told her.

Sophie was a poor Catholic girl and had worked as a maid for a wealthy Jewish family in Poland before the war, and when the Nazis came they killed the family she worked for, but she managed to sneak the youngest son, Mickey, out of his house while his family was being rounded up, and she hid him in her own house and then claimed him as her own son. She kept him safe all during the war, pretending to be his mother, and when the war ended she took him on the first boat to Palestine, because she wanted to find his relatives there and raise him with their help as a Jew as his mother would have wished. But, although grateful that she had saved him, Mickey's relatives were appalled at the idea of him being raised by a Catholic woman. And a maid, at that. They promised her money for passage to Canada and a job in Vancouver if she would leave Mickey alone. She did not want to do this, but they were adamant. He was already too attached. This was their condition. So she left him there and came to Vancouver. She wrote him letters, but either the family apprehended them or he never bothered to write back. Either way, it broke her heart. She kept hoping someday to find him again. She went to the Jewish community center, asking for help. They knew Sophie was one of the righteous gentiles, gentiles who had saved Jews during the war, and they found Mickey for her and raised money to bring him to Vancouver for a surprise reunion. Of course, to her he was still her son, but to him she was just a distant memory from a long time ago. An unhappy and frightening time. He was grateful and kind, but it was clear that he was relieved when it was time to leave again for Israel.

Afterward, she ran into Mrs. Mendelbaum in her building and recognized her from the Jewish community center. Sophie had kept Mickey in her heart all these years as her son, but now she saw that he was not. That truly she had no family. And Mrs. Mendelbaum had just lost the last member of her family. So they struck up a friendship and on Fridays went to the center to make bread together. When Mrs. Mendelbaum moved to the island, Sophie was frantic. She thought that Mrs. Mendelbaum had put herself in a very precarious position and she didn't know what to do. She was making herself ill with worry and had even gone to the police, but, of course, the police politely dismissed her, so she went to her priest, Father John Humdinger. Humdinger told Dr. Houseman that he thought Sophie half hoped he *would* find something wrong, so that Mrs. Mendelbaum would have to return to Vancouver. He promised to go to the island and make sure Mrs. Mendelbaum was all right, to check out the situation and have a talk with Marten Knockers without telling Marten Knockers that he was a priest. No one, *absolutely no one*, Sophie emphasized, must know that he was Father John, or Mrs. Mendelbaum would be furious.

It was going to be tricky, Humdinger thought, explaining his presence on the island to Marten Knockers. In desperation he had even thought he might tell Marten Knockers that he was there to sell encyclopedias. This, he later understood when he knew Marten Knockers better, would have worked just fine. But, fortunately, he never had to use it because Mrs. Mendelbaum solved the problem almost immediately by hiring him as the butler. He would let Uncle assume he had come for the interview and then decided not to take the job, and in the meantime he'd fulfill his promise to Sophie by ascertaining that all was well with Mrs. Mendelbaum. But all didn't seem to be well with Mrs. Mendelbaum. He looked around and saw the stopped-up sink, the near-hysterical Mrs. Mendelbaum, the two recently orphaned girls, and Uncle Marten, who seemed to be in over his head, and he decided that for a while, at least, perhaps the island was where he was needed. So he wrote his bishop and got permission to take the vacation time he had not taken for twenty years, and kept his collar turned, and stayed. He had a younger priest come and take over his duties at the street shelter for runaways where he worked part-time and from where he knew Dr. Houseman, who came in one morning a week to work in the adjoining free clinic. And when I got ill, he called her.

I asked Dr. Houseman why Sophie was so adamant about not revealing Father John's identity. Dr. Houseman said it was because Mrs. Mendelbaum hated how Sophie went on and on about wonderful Father John. She thought Sophie was besotted. One day she got fed up and banned any more conversation about him ever again. And Sophie did not want to lose the friendship. So Mrs. Mendelbaum must not find out that Sophie had sent the banned Father John to check on her.

The only question I had left was the bull. What about the bull, I asked Uncle Marten later. "What bull?" he asked abstractedly.

So I never found out about the bull. Or really knew much more about Humdinger than that, but I did find out that Uncle was right and Dr. Houseman had been in love with Humdinger. I finally got her to admit it to me when she said that soon she would be leaving the island and moving to help open clinics in small towns in Manitoba. "But won't you miss Humdinger?" I asked craftily. She said that I must promise never to mention it again, especially not around Humdinger, whom it might make uncomfortable if he knew, but because she was leaving soon she would admit she had loved Humdinger even though she knew nothing could come of it, but even that didn't bother her because she didn't attach to anyone that way. That when she was with them it was fine and when she wasn't that was fine, too. That it was a detached kind of love.

Several days later when I brought Mrs. Mendelbaum a tray as a favor to Humdinger, Dr. Houseman was leaving her room with a bottle of the cough medicine in her hand. Mrs. Mendelbaum was mad at Dr. Houseman, who was confiscating the cough syrup and meeting with Sophie to find out what went in it, because although she had dismissed it originally as just a harmless herbal home remedy, she was puzzled by why Mrs. Mendelbaum and Jocelyn continued to go about in a daze and before she left for Manitoba she was going to make sure that the medicine was indeed harmless and so tie up any loose ends. But even if Mrs. Mendelbaum hadn't been annoyed with Dr. Houseman about this, I knew she didn't think much of her.

"She has no understanding, that one," said Mrs. Mendelbaum. "She has compassion but no empathy."

I told her what Dr. Houseman had said to me about not being attached, and Mrs. Mendelbaum said, "That is not to love. To love, you make the pact with the universe that someday separated from this person you will be and destroyed by such loss but this you are willing to do, knowing that love comes at such a cost. If no other miracles we see, that we do this over and over, this agreement at such a price—shain vi di zibben velten, heldish. But detached love, ech, no such thing. Love is bound to this end, all else is only kindness."

I went to Jocelyn's room after that. I was talking to her every day now. She was still pretty groggy and out of it most of the time, but I kept her updated.

It took Jocelyn a long time to get off the medicine. Mrs. Mendelbaum never did. She did not want a new beginning. She had had enough. She had not the energy for it. Her heart was left behind with her four dead sons and husband. The time when she had been so quietly happy. We tried to make things comfortable for her anyway, and I think we did. And at the end there was Humdinger, Jocelyn, Sophie, and myself beside her when she said, "Sof kol sof," with weary decision and died.

Because I wanted to know what Mrs. Mendelbaum's last words had meant, it occurred to me that I could learn Yiddish. I was sorry I hadn't thought of this earlier, that year when I could not make new beginnings, but now I learned from Sophie, who was glad to have a hobby. I learned:

Ganz kaput—completely broken
Alter kucker—lecherous old man
G'vir—rich man
Gut far him—serves him right
Er zol vaksen vi a tsibeleh, mit dem kop in
    drerd—he should grow like an onion, with
    his head in the ground
Ich hob es in drerd—to hell with it
Farkuckt—dung-y
Meshugeh—crazy
Shmek tabik—nothing of value
Es past nit—it is not becoming
Kaput—broken, gone
Tsedrait—screwy
Es brent mir ahfen hartz—I have heartburn
Hert zich ein—listen here
Got in himmel—God in heaven
A feier zol im trefen—he should burn up
A brocheh—a blessing
Ahzes ponim—impudent fellow
Bal toyreh—learned man
Ganz farmutshet—completely exhausted
Me ken brechen—you can vomit from this
Goyishe—gentile
Shmaltz—fat

Loz mich tzu ru—leave me alone

Shtetl—village

Az a yor ahf mir—I should have such good luck

Kabaret forshtelung—floor show

Gelibteh—beloved

Sitzfleish—patience that can endure sitting

Ich zol azoy vissen fun tzores—I should know as little about trouble

Kaddishel—term of endearment for a boy or man

Maideleh—affectionate term for a girl

Es iz a shandeh far di kinder—it's a shame for the children

Tahkeh a metsieh—really a bargain (sarcastic)

Es vet gornit helfen—nothing will help

Pyesseh—a drama

Meshugener—crazy male

Shain vi di zibben velten—beautiful as the seven worlds

Heldish—brave

Sof kol sof—let's end it

And finally what Sophie said back to Mrs. Mendelbaum when she said sof kol sof: alaichem sholom—to you be peace.